LOVE AND A DOZEN ROAST POTATOES

LOVE
AND A DOZEN
ROAST
POTATOES

*(One man's honest tale
of impossible romance and
coconut rum regret.)*

by
SIMON WAN

URBANE
Publications

urbanepublications.com

First published in Great Britain in 2016 by Urbane Publications Ltd
Suite 3, Brown Europe House, 33/34 Gleaming Wood Drive, Chatham, Kent ME5 8RZ
Copyright © Simon Wan, 2016

A CIP catalogue record for this book is available from the British Library.

ISBN 978-1-910692-90-5
Kindle 978-1-910692-92-9
EPUB 978-1-910692-91-2

Design and Typeset by Julie Martin
Cover by Julie Martin

Printed and bound by CPI Group (UK) Ltd, Croydon, CR0 4YY

urbanepublications.com

This book is dedicated to my grandfather Harry for my jawline and my mother Jacqui for my love of roast potatoes.

Acknowledgements

I'd like to thank perfect smiles, tattooed ravers, the man in the hat, the boy with the big nose, the girl who went to sleep, eyes that change colour, chilled out brick layers, electro cat lovers, posh school film nerds, frame making disc jockeys, mentors that repeat themselves, couples that dance in France, beekeeping rockers, money making mods, the godson who stayed ginger, his dad who saved my life, victoria sponge bakers, risk taking book lovers, crazy tigers, my family in the west, my family in the east, moon river roll ups that smoulder on boats, magical elves that eat noodles in the bath and finally my stuntman brother Martin for turning out awesome, even though he made me ride my moped into town to rent 'Care Bears: The Movie' a hundred times, possibly more.

Foreword

The strongest image in my mind from the first few years of my life are of a shining beacon of rebellion and beauty. Princess Leia. She was sassy, and she knew her way around a blaster. No pun intended, we're starting from the very beginning, so no hot sauce until I'm at least 16, and when I say hot sauce I mean sex …

1.

Ifirst became aware of the difference between girls and boys not via the usual channels – toy bias, pink clothes for Sarah and blue for Steve – but by having a very ambiguous seventies bob haircut. People used to point at me a lot. It's probably one of the reasons I love Stevie Wonder's "Isn't she lovely". I just gave in and accepted that I looked like a pretty little chubby Chinese girl. At least I was pretty, and we all know how important that is. Having dealt with my sexual ambiguity at an early age and being allowed to play with dolls as well as machine guns I came armed with a fairly well rounded sense of play. I loved playing with my polystyrene Spitfire just as much as I loved dressing up in a gold curtain and walking around my bedroom listening to the theme music from Grease.

"Is he a boy or a girl? English or Chinese?" Questions I could see flash in the eyes of the grown-ups that towered over me curiously as a child. Having nearly reached the male milestone of forty, I can say with some truth that I'm now one of those adults asking myself the same question in the bathroom mirror. Is there anything weird about standing in the bathroom staring at yourself asking questions? Nope. That's just something to do when you're brushing your teethie pegs. A weirder thing to do in a bathroom would be to coax a five-year-old boy into it with a multi coloured beach ball and then show him your rude bits. Which is exactly what happened to me.

Don't worry. There wasn't a radio DJ in sight, rather a gang of five-year-old girls wearing deelie boppers and drinking orange out of plastic cups. It seemed like so much fun. Innocent exploration and children testing their own boundaries, nothing more, nothing perverted. It was basically doctors and nurses, but I was the only boy. I remember standing there with my shorts around my ankles, laughing that they didn't have a willy. I heard my Mum calling over the hysterical giggles and they panicked!

"Why is the door locked? OPEN THE DOOR!"

At the time I remember thinking my mum was over-reacting. I never thought that five-year-old kids shouldn't lock themselves in a room with running water and poisonous solvents. I was having way too much fun. As my lovely Mum was telling me off seconds later, I remember thinking, "Girls, are funny. I think I like them…"

The very first girl I fell in love with was called Claire, I was eight years old. Dark shiny hair like a polished space helmet with big brown eyes and bright red shoes with a silver buckle. I met her one lunch time with her blonde friend and we went to the end of the playing field to pick blackberries. She liked me because she said I was rubbish at football.

At first I thought that it was a bit of a mean thing to say. I am, and always have been a very physical person but I never got the point of kicking a ball. I mean, where would that ever lead anyone?

As I picked berries with them both giggling, I could hear a couple of the boys shouting names. I had only been at the school for a couple of days and being a half-Chinese in the eighties was admittedly unusual. Claire and Blondie thought that a kiss on the cheek would make me feel better. With the clanging of the playtime bell, as we made our way back, I stopped on the edge of the football pitch for a moment, while twenty or so flailing idiots chased a bag of air.

One of the boys shouted something silly, a top insult for an eight-year-old won't really have gravitas here, but what happened next probably set the precedent for the next thirty-two years. They both kissed me on the cheek, one on each side, right there in front of all the boys in my class. The next playtime, the boys who called me 'chinky-chong pong face' were a little more interested in being my friend. I spent the next few weeks being 'cool'. I was the exotic new kid in town with TWO girlfriends. I was on fire.

Two weeks of being top boy made me feel giddy. I never liked getting up for school but at least now while I was there it was pretty much having a laugh, picking fruit, getting kisses on the cheek and then lunch. The rest of the day being made up of mainly shouting, lots of felt tip pens and leaning back in your chair. It was very important to be able to lean quite far back. It was instant attention from the powers that be.

"You'll end up in the hospital DEAD!" (It was the Eighties.)

Everyone turned to look, would the shock of the teacher's outburst tip me over? Would I snap back to attention like a good little Eighties robot boy? I think it's generally a bad thing to always have something to say. You run the risk of talking shit all the time and that's off putting and annoying for everyone. On this occasion the words that came out of my mouth were a surprise. If you examine the phrase in any depth, it doesn't really make that much of a point, but when I said:

"...and how will I walk there if I'm dead!" Smug.

I got a laugh. My two girlfriends giggled at my amazing turn of phrase. The boys loved my dangerous chair leaning skills and the teacher sucked up my wit with a wink. Never mind on fire, I was a fucking hero.

I never worried about getting told off about things I did at school. At the time we were living at my Nan's house so it was like a holiday and a family visit rolled into one. You can never really get in trouble if you live at your Grandparents house, it's some kind of child protection law for kids born in the Seventies. With my cocky shine glistening in the spring morning air, I felt great. Untouchable. Today was going to be even better. I'd been practicing some good leaning in my Grandma's kitchen, my Grandad would let me do it as it annoyed her. I could almost remain suspended on two legs for the count of ten. My imagination piqued. The classroom was waiting for me.

The world crash zoomed. I stumbled. Tight frizzy dark brown curls of hair. He looked like an old man even at eight years old. My uniform was a mix and match of what I'd had at my previous school (of which there are many). No one cared, I had two girlfriends and the teacher liked my cheek. He cared. He cared so much that he was sat in my spot. My spot where I was at some point, probably after lunch, going to drop a ten-second-no-handed- two-legged-chair-lean and everyone will cheer. Who the flip was this dude? He looked like he was dressed by the people who did the C&A shop window, he was spotless and boring. His pencil case had a flip-out pencil sharpener and he was laughing, and the boys were laughing and the girls were laughing and the teacher was laughing and everyone thought this boy was hilarious. I thought that something was going on, I'd seen 'Tales of the Unexpected' one night through a crack in the front room door and thought maybe it was to do with that kind of thing.

There was only one place to sit. Right opposite my old spot. Now this wasn't a problem, I'll sit anywhere, but it meant my two girlfriends were now sat either side of him and not me. They were leaning into him! The cheek of it, I was going to lean NOT them! As the teacher called my name, there was a sound. Before I could yell to confirm my existence at the very top of my voice, there was a little sarcastic chuckle and booming from opposite me came the words, "THE PIE MAN!"

Kapow.

The room exploded. This kid had game.

Even the teacher paused to hear my reaction. It was almost as if I had permission to prove myself. It turned out this kid wasn't a new kid like me. No, he'd just been away for a few weeks. Everyone knew him already. The girls covered their faces, they were my girls, they knew they were, but you can't argue with 'The pie man!'. They tried so hard not to keep giggling. Not straight after Teacher says "Simon". I was dead in the water. The boys weren't so apologetic, they wanted a battle. It was a rap battle for sprogs.

"You're called curly head wee wee head."

Jab.

"Why are you from Ping Pong Land?"

Technical.

"At least I come from a Land."

Geographic, back foot.

"Your jumper's brown like dog and cow poo."

Low blow.

It was true, my jumper wasn't dark blue like his. I needed more than words, I'd never met another boy who was so quick-witted. In a split second he made me question if I really was from Ping Pong land at all. I needed the big guns, actions always speak louder than words.

As the teacher light-heartedly down-palmed the tittering, he made his way to our table. Stopping behind this rapscallion, he turned away from us, putting up a poster on the wall. It would take him around ten seconds. The perfect amount of time. All I needed was ten seconds and the room would be all mine again. This was the time to strike, all eyes on me. I whispered as loudly and as menacingly as I could.

"Yeah, well because you don't know about THIS!"

With a flourish I grabbed his pencil case and pushed my chair back. With a single shove I jostled my body into perfect balance. With his pencil case in my outstretched flailing right arm I was leaning on my chair without a care in the world. Ten seconds was all I needed. The moment was too strong. The weight of the pencil case gave me an added level of control I'd never experienced before. I could lean so far back and then forward I felt like a Jedi. I was dancing, dancing on two legs. It was incredible.

When I threw the pencil case at his face, it was mainly due to a surge of heightened mania. The mood certainly changed. I'd thrown it just as the teacher was turning round. So what he saw was me on my chair waving my arms and throwing things in a classmate's face. He wasn't impressed. He looked disappointed more than anything. He made it into a lesson, and had a little talk about anger. Why you shouldn't throw things at people's faces. I think I got him quite good, but this time action did speak louder than words. Maybe he'll back down now. I can't face this every day; school's about laughing and kissing, not war. We were made to shake hands. I'd seen this in films so I stood up. I waited. He leaned forward with hand outstretched. I was standing up offering my hand and he couldn't be bothered to even meet me halfway. Screw this! The last trickle of adrenalin flicked my little balls.

I shouted, "Scared to touch what you can't afford!". Cocky slap.

"Claire said you don't play football because you're from Ching Chong Chinaman". A devastating blow.

"I bet I can kick better than you. You're a stupid joey deacon spastic face." Full contortions. Cacky hands.

The thing I should have paid attention to, ironically, in the midst of my fascination with chairs and their various angles, was the chair he was sitting on. As Teacher pulled the beige Parka from behind my enemy, I noticed his chair had handles. What the flip was this about, and why were my two girlfriends giving me a funny look. It was like they thought I'd done something really bad, like when instead of saving some berries for Claire's cake shop near the hopscotch, Blondie and I made paint with them and covered a whole strip of fence in purple while she waited by the sandpit for her ingredients. This time, they were all doing it. I had no idea why. I found out exactly ten seconds later.

He'd been born with a severe degenerative muscle defect and had been away recovering from another round of surgery. The outcome of which would make his life less painful but unable to walk again unaided as an adult. The teacher wheeled him out of the classroom because he started to cry and thought he may like some privacy. I looked up at the poster the teacher had put up. It was a picture of the boy in hospital, tubes and nurses all around him smiling. The words, 'GOOD LUCK' and 'WE'LL MISS YOU' cut out of silver paper and stuck on it.

As I sat there the air was certainly frostier than before, but when I look back, two girlfriends at eight years old was probably a bit too much anyway.

2.

At nine years old, I felt most comfortable wearing nothing but polyester action shorts. Black with speed stripes down each side for extra boost and a secret pocket for treasure. White socks pulled up high. Black plimsolls and some kind of weapon made out of stolen wood, elastic bands and a nail, rusty if possible for extra effect. Sometimes it got heavy out there but it was also hot when I was a boy, too hot for tracksuits. Not like now. It was hot every summer and all summer so I wore my shorts. All the time.

Standing on a new playground on the first day of a new school year, I toyed with the idea of telling someone I didn't like football. The boys at my last school knew they could pick me last and I wouldn't feel bad and the teacher wouldn't have to care about making them be fair. There were three of us left. Me in the middle and two girls either side. Mixed football? I should have clicked straight away. I wasn't sure if the sticker books everyone loved were filled with just men or women or both? Something wasn't right and I didn't need a crack in the door to see it. The girls looked at me embarrassed. Giggling either side of me. When I asked what was funny, the reply was focused on my shorts. Okay, straight in, easy. They were probably thinking that with my amazing shorts and my sporty frame that I was actually great at football, and that by not picking me the team who lost out would look like idiots. I chuckled and offered that it was okay, I actually wasn't that good at football so they don't even need to worry about it. One of the girls offered back that I talked stupid and had a bum like a girl. Apparently I had a chunky lower half and my tight black shorts were in need of an update. Everyone laughed in my direction. Pointing. All pointing at my muscular thighs. My shorts were short for a reason. I'd spent all summer doing intense Kung Fu horse stance with my friend who lived opposite my Nan, and practicing full-speed skids on my bike. I could jump a plank and do curbs on roller skates but that was just for fun. My legs were flipping powerful and I wanted everyone to know it.

This place was hostile. Suburban. At the end of this playground there wasn't a secret oasis of fruit waiting to be picked in the afternoon sun, but a criss-cross fence with a narrow walkway running along the whole length. The walkway was also made of a criss- cross fence which made the whole panorama look a little bit like an old war film prison camp, but in Eighties colours. I was about to enter a world of folded paper notes where you can meet a girl, fall in love and get dumped in the time it takes for your coat to miss the peg and drop to the floor. It was fast. It was dangerous. I saw a kid nearly drown. The best basketball player in the whole school split his head open on a radiator. It was deadly. There was fighting, there was running, there was hiding. The second best thing about this place was that when the girls chased you and caught you, they kissed you. But the first best thing about this place was Katrina.

It was the hair I noticed first. It was so bright she looked like an actual doll. More a Cindy than a Barbie I thought, with perhaps a touch of Sylvanian Families in her dress. She was always in class before me and she was always happy to see me. She'd make a point of showing me she'd saved my seat, even though we sat there every day. I only ever remember one thing she said as every time I looked at her I saw rainbows and my hearing went thumpy. She made everything sparkle. I liked sitting next to her. Some of the other boys made jokes. The same ones as before. They called me Bruce Lee, or said that my Dad worked in a restaurant. Which I realised wasn't really offensive as it was true. The older boys couldn't get to me. I didn't give a toss about being called a Kung Fu legend or having loads of free amazing food. Nope, every day in class I'd be sat next to Katrina and everything would be lovely. I wasn't picking fruit but I was getting kissed a lot during high octane kiss chase at play time, so just sitting next to her was all I needed. The first time her chair was empty I thought I was early for a change. I was quite chuffed with myself. I'd save a chair for her this time. How unexpected. I couldn't wait for her to appear and I'd copy her little wave and act all bossy like girls generally do and tell her to hurry up and sit down. It was a few months before she sat next to me again, it felt like ages. One of my friends had said that our teacher told them where Katrina had gone but he couldn't remember, something complicated and foreign.

As we were putting our chairs up at the end of the day, one of the other girls in the class asked me why my eyes

looked different, so I told her. My Dad was from Kong
Kong and my Mum was from Wembley. This fascinated
her, she had lived in the same house all her life. This
fascinated me, I'd never stopped moving. I told her about
all the weird things that I'd heard about Hong Kong. All
the Oriental magic and the food in the streets. I told her
about what it was like living in Ireland for a couple of
years. I told her school was quite easy there. They finished
at half-past two and in the summer I played croquet with
the Major of Dalkey's granddaughters in my pyjamas. She
told me that she wanted to be rich and have loads of new
outfits. We played kiss chase together. She was feisty, she
was nimble she would dominate all areas of running after
boys, catching boys and doing things to boys. If it was
going down, Kelly would know about it. I was certainly
in the minority being a boy who liked getting caught, but
every so often for fun I unleashed my insane speed (my
legs were still chunky, but they'd all forgotten) and I'd spin
and dodge and the boys would have to accept that I was
a little bit tasty. They'd all be wiping their faces in disgust
and the girls would be laughing like miniature cartoon
witches and I'd be doing cartwheels through swathes of
hair bobbles and gingham without even the slightest touch.
It was acrobatic, but it was the same every day. The secret
game of letting the cute ones catch you soon got tiresome.
I didn't play football, and the best basketball player in the
school was so good, he could beat all the playground by
himself. I wanted something exciting to happen.

The kids here were pretty well organised, it was
under control. Kelly made up the majority of playground

activities for our little gang, usually involving cartwheels, chasing, boys and yes … kissing them. As we were good buddies I could ask her to pick a certain girl; you know, if she looked extra cute that day. As I glanced like a tiny Hugh Hefner over the playground, with Kelly waiting for me to pick, my view was ruined. Some nutter was riding his bike on the field. That wasn't allowed, it wasn't going home time. He had a group of boys running after him, hyenas, frothy-mouthed and looking for trouble. The boy on the bike executed a perfect skid in front of me. Arc of dust. He stepped over the bike and stopped, his stooped head six inches away from my face.

"What you looking at?" Aggressive.

"Girls for kiss cha…" I was on the floor.

The cheek of it was that he really shouldn't have been riding his bike on the field in the first place. It threw me. He rode a Bomber, which meant it was a big bike. He had a big bike because he was big. He was the biggest boy in the school and for some reason he wanted to beat me up using judo. I think it was a misplaced Eastern thing, Japanese and half-Chinese look very similar if all you have to go by is nothing. He was fair. He let me get up. Everyone was shouting and the word 'fight' became a cacophony. Now I'm not a tall man and it's fair to say I haven't shrunk, therefore I wasn't a big kid. What I lacked in height I made up for in noise, and what I lacked in strength I made up for with my version of Kung Fu. What did they know? It was years until Jackie Chan would even make a tinkle in Hollywood, let alone an industrial town in the South of England.

It had worked for me previously. A few days before, I was sat with Katrina on a little brick flower bed after lunch when the whole school started screaming. It was sharp. A scream without laughter, it was one purely made up of pain. Someone had discovered how to do a 'Chinese Burn'. It got around pretty fast that if your arms were showing, you're "gunna get burned". Katrina was wearing a dress with no sleeves. Easy target. I knew I had to protect her. The screams became louder and in a blur of cardigans we were both surrounded by a cluster of boys with red raw arms, each one gagging to pass on the searing hot twisting torture. No one was going to touch Katrina, she was made of pure sunshine and everything from the ice cream van. I gritted my teeth and rolled back my sleeves. It all went quiet. All I could feel was Katrina, her face buried in my side, her eyes clenched. All I could hear was the panting of the hyenas, a strange moment. The screaming had stopped. They were unsure. After all it was called a 'Chinese Burn'.

"It won't work on me 'cause I'm half Chinese so you might as well don't bother." Shot in the dark.

This stumped the pain-hungry flock.

"How do we know it doesn't work?" Fair point.

Katrina didn't really raise her voice much, she nattered on about things and laughed and giggled but it was like a melodious chime. Then she said, "Cause if you do it on him it won't even hurt a single teeny bit that's how come!"

Ah. It was definitely a shout.

Now I knew what she was trying to do. I know. It was brilliant really. It's just that she said it as a challenge.

If she'd delivered the line more casually they may have been fooled. By now their thirst for pain had become an insatiable curiosity. Would a Chinese burn actually hurt me? I didn't know and they didn't know either. You needed two hands to get the full ripping scorch so obviously I wouldn't have tried it on myself. Besides, I'd only just found out what they were.

The crowd became much more cajoling. Rather than throwing punches they were throwing reasons why I should let them give me a Chinese burn. It became quite political. Who would do it, and why? Should they pick for twisting strength or longest fingers? Which way? How long for? Over the elbow or near the wrist? Hard to get perfect in the eight minutes since it had been going around the school yard. So many points of view. They were just arguing amongst themselves. Even I got involved, some of what they were saying was ridiculous. There was no way it would make me left-handed and there was no chance it would make the blood vessels in my willy explode. I could see quite clearly the marks on all the other boys' arms, they were all still standing, and more because it was just annoying I stuck my arm out.

"Just do it then!" In for a penny.

It hurt so much I felt like Luke Skywalker when his Dad cut his hand off but I couldn't let them know. They were examining my facial expressions for any sign of tears or wincing. It felt like the skin was ripping and a scorching band of fire wrapped around my forearm. Katrina was confident, she had her arms crossed and her pretty face scrunched up in a scowl. Her grit was infectious. Before when I looked at her she was a little angel that you'd put on top of your tree, now she was a rock. If she believed it, then I did too. We locked eyes in team spirit as they twisted my arm, her face demanding that I don't give in and as soon as it started, it stopped. I hadn't even said a word. Katrina smiled at me. The crowd was impressed. Eventually I felt a bit left out. All of a sudden you'd hear a cry of "Chinese Burns!", a gang of boys scrambling for victims and girls running away covering their arms and I'd just sit and wait until they all came back.

"Sorry mate, but it don't work on you." Left out.

Apparently the big boy on the bike standing over me now had heard the Chinese Burn story and that I couldn't feel pain because my Dad was from Hong Kong. I had some kind of invincible power, he'd heard that Chinese burns didn't work on me, pulling my hair was pointless and if you bit me you'd get soy sauce in your mouth. If I was in his shoes, I admit I'd have been curious as well. Whichever way you looked at it, there was going to be a fight. He was obviously bigger than me but I could see in his eyes he wasn't sure. He swung a haymaker over the top of my head – being smaller wasn't always a bad thing. I'd love to say it was a designed defence. I'd love to say that I knew exactly what I was doing. The truth of the actual throw down was more that the momentum of his crazy swing threw him off balance and he toppled on top of me. I'd just wanted to get the heck out of the way. My attempt of making a quick exit coupled with his angry swinging fists created a dance, that to the casual observer looked exactly like I'd just Judo'd the heck out of him and smashed him face-first into the floor in front of the whole school. I was just as surprised as he was. Even the dinner lady had her hand over her mouth. I could see that no one knew what to do, it was tense. I didn't want to fight. As far as I was concerned I was in the middle of choosing a new girl for kiss chase and the next thing I knew I had flipped the biggest kid in school over my shoulder and he was slumped on the ground next to his massive bike. I remembered how one teacher I had made us shake hands. It showed respect, compassion and the hope that he'd calm down. I held out my hand and luckily he reached up and took it. He looked quite pleased with himself. It turns out that no one had ever flipped him like that. He asked me if it was some kind of secret Chinese martial arts. I told him it was, obviously. By now a few of the teachers had arrived and the crowds were shuffling back to the natural order of the playground leaving me with my little Harem. Kelly was in charge of the games, I knew this, but as I waited for her to decide what we were playing next, she looked at me and waited. This was weird. I was glad that I'd luckily escaped a beating in front of everyone but also aware that my position of power in the playground had shifted slightly. It was exciting.

Power is a funny thing. The ability to say something and then watch someone do that thing is odd. I didn't need sweets or football stickers, so my powers didn't affect the boys. I could respond fast and convincingly when confronted with a question while clearly not listening, so my powers didn't affect the teachers. I was already hanging out with the best girls in my class. I couldn't think

of any ways to test my new position on the playground.
Kelly gave up waiting. I was frankly a letdown. Until …
one lunch time, Kelly and I had a great idea for a game.

I don't think it lasted long enough to have a name. If
it did, I can't remember it. After just explaining it to one
of my housemates he said two words, 'Tit Chase'. Cheers
Tony. Tit Chase is not completely accurate but does give the
gist. I had invented a game in which I picked all the cutest
girls, the ones that were pretty, or could do handstands, or
had a great impression, or who knew the words to 'Wham
Rap' or always had a slice of real pineapple in her lunch
box. They were the elite. Me? I was just lucky. The game
went like this:

1. The boys ran away.
2. The girls chased them.
3. When a boy was caught, they had to let the girls kiss
   them.
4. When I was caught, the girls had to flash me their
   bra.

The only girl who was wearing anything near a bra was
Kelly. The reason I knew she had one was because she
seemed very pleased with herself and told me. The other
girls were in awe. Something was going to happen to the
girls in our class and it involved strappy elastic stuff. She
was training apparently. I always liked Kelly's spirit. It was
this kind of pre-planning and attention to detail that made
being with her fun. I am aware that the game sounds a

little PG for a primary school but I urge you to remember I was only little. My favourite clothes were mainly neon, covered in badges and I drew a lot of 'Ghostbusters' posters for my friends Ronnie and Paul. I was normal. It wasn't seedy.

I had used my new found influence to spend more time alone with Kelly without even realising it. I looked forward to our own private version of our little 'game'. It would run like this.

1. Kelly and I would run off giggling.
2. She'd flash me.
3. We'd kiss each other on the cheek.
4. We'd run away from each other laughing.

I think I was her first 'proper' boyfriend. When I heard the song 'You to me are everything', I had the urge to draw a rose with my new felt tip pens. This was intense.

• • •

I went to Hong Kong for the first time shortly after. I was excited to get back to the UK so I could give Katrina a red and gold paper fan that I'd bought in a steamy late night street market. When I said goodbye to her on my last day of school before I left for the East, she looked like her batteries had run out but she was determined to make a fuss about me going on a jumbo jet. Listing do's and don'ts like the glamorous air hostesses we'd seen on Blue

Peter. I wondered if she was okay.

"Don't forget to get me a stick of rock." A little worn out smile.

I didn't even know if they had rock in Hong Kong.

"What colour?"

I watched her pout and think.

"Red and gold." Always shiny.

She wasn't there when I got back. It must have been ages now since I'd seen her. Never mind I'd just leave it in her drawer, she'll find it and wonder how it got there; yes, this was even better. My teacher saw me opening Katrina's drawer and came over. He said that I wasn't in trouble but that Katrina wasn't feeling very well, and as I was her sit-next-to-in-class-best-friend that I should know first. Phew, I thought I was about to get in trouble as it may have looked like I was stealing, even though it was the opposite. It was even more cool because if she had been feeling poorly, a surprise Chinese fan from a market would make her explode in little giggles and sunshine bubbles. Which is way better than being ill. I knew I'd nailed the colours, there being no seaside rock in Hong Kong it was a lucky alternative.

Kelly had never had silk purse before. She was excited about the present even before she opened it. Inside the little pink and white single button purse was a green stone trinket on a red silk string. Nothing expensive. I felt like a pirate, she'd never seen mystical jade before, and especially not from the other side of the world. I had an extra bounce in my step as I walked home. I was chuffed that Kelly loved her surprise and even more happy about the thought of Katrina getting to class early and finding her paper fan that I kept in my back pack all the way from Hong Kong. Things were different now. We stayed in this town for much longer than anywhere before. Normally it was me that disappeared overnight, but this time it was my sit-next-to-in-class-best-friend who never came back. I spent the next few weeks wondering where she was until my friend Ronnie showed me his skateboard and I forgot all about girls – even Kelly and her bra, even Katrina and her red and gold fan. I swapped the delicate smell of bubble bath and strawberry sweets for the sound of thunder on concrete, and kisses on the cheek for blood and bruises.

3.

When I found out we were moving again it wasn't a big surprise. I was thirteen years old and by now had a little brother. This time I had about a month's notice. We were leaving the skateboard heaven they call Milton Keynes and moving to the cobbled Midlands to open a takeaway. Even though I believed that this would be the end of my skateboarding dream I was excited about the thought of living in a takeaway. All that food. The one thing that I think made the bond with my little brother so strong was our love of tasty things, and Kung Fu. So, with a whole Chinese takeaway at our fingertips it's a miracle that we're not both chunky buggers and a blessing that we get on so well. It wasn't such a big deal for him that we were moving, he was three. He was way more interested in Roland Rat, our two cats and bombing around the kitchen on a plastic red truck. It wasn't a big deal for me either really. By now we'd moved town at least nine times. But should I tell my friends I was leaving or keep it a secret? One friend in particular.

I thought she looked French. She had a certain swish about her that made me feel funny in my guts. The other boys in my class said they wouldn't go near her because she's young and won't know what to do. I wonder what they thought we should be doing at thirteen years old in the Eighties. The options were yo-yo's, skateboards, neon laces or Police Academy. Or there was the park. The park after school. I got teased by so many of my friends because I'd want to walk home with girls. The boys wanted to talk about football or fight. I hated football and they were always scared that my secret Chinese mixed-blood would equal martial arts death if they messed with me so it was boring and they all smelled musty after a day running around chasing balls. Girls on the other hand smelled nice. They liked little shiny things. Things that you wrap up in knots, things that you could stick on your bag, things that made your tongue go pink, all kinds of weird stuff. I loved music. I loved singing and dancing, but trying to get the lads to stop playing 'keepie-uppies' to see if your moonwalk is getting better never went down that well. The sweet smelling shiny girls, they loved that shit. They had magazines, tape recorders and the whole fucking works. Plus, they always had spare pencils and paper and generally things you needed.

But I digress. To me she was the prettiest girl in the year below. Light brown hair that fell loose to her shoulders and an oval face with green eyes. Maybe because she was a year younger or maybe because she didn't care, she wasn't covered in neon pink make-up with 'Boy George' written on her face with biro. She looked clean and soft and warm and hopeful. To a thirteen-year-old boy it wasn't just that she was pretty. It was the things she did. The way she laughed, the way she sighed, the way she thought I was funny, the way she stayed at the park with me on the swings until the very last second before her Dad would start shouting from the back door across the field;

and most importantly, the way she kissed me on the lips to say thanks after I rescued her from a local tooled up gang.

They'd surrounded her under the slide. I saw her sitting neatly, trying not to look scared, standing her ground. They had sticks and were banging the chunky wooden beams that made the little roof shudder. The clang had a metallic edge as the vibrations shook through the slide above. I caught her eye as I edged closer. Five boys, five sticks. They were in the year below, but still, five against one is a 'chef's gamble'. I'm basically going to lose. The gang turned to see who she was looking at.

Flipping Hell! It was that big kid from the new estate. What was he doing here? We'd crossed paths before. I kicked him in the chest once while we were all outside on the school playing field. Someone was getting an award and we had to clap. The teachers were talking to Anita Dobson from EastEnders. She was the surprise celebrity guest and sang a blustery treble heavy version of 'Anyone can fall in love' which is the theme tune. They had a rocket car on the grass and apart from getting in trouble when he had an asthma attack, it was a wicked day. He'd said that EastEnders was rubbish and that only old ladies watched it. I told him that he was incorrect, that it was actually a refreshing look at modern Britain and that if we dissect each of the main characters' individual wants and desir … no. Actually I just kicked him in the chest and he collapsed in front of Angie Watts. It was because of this particular day, as he span around and glared at me, that I felt he wanted to prove a point.

I told myself that the reason I wasn't going to tell her

I was leaving town was because it was funny. What a clever joke. It excited me to keep it a secret from her, even though I did have to tell a few people I was off. I swore them to lower year secrecy so she'd never find out. What a hilarious jape. The joke would run like this:

1. The Girl would ask where the Boy is?
2. The Girls and Boys in the year above would tell her, "He moved away to another town."
3. The Girl would laugh and everyone makes friends.
4. The Girl would in no way feel humiliated or at the very least confused and disappointed in the actions of her year above Boyfriend.

I did want to tell her, but the idea of a goodbye actually made me feel weird. The ceremony of a last goodbye just seemed messy. I couldn't see the point. I was moving away, get used to it, see you later. I knew from experience that I'd probably end up hanging out with the kids who liked to muck about. Standard. Playing on my new kid shtick I wasn't scared of facing hundreds of new kids and another round of welcoming biscuit-smelling teachers. Easy. Finding another girl to sit with me on the swings. Shit. What if they aren't as nice as she was. Shit. I was going to … something. Something like, wanting to see her. No matter how far away I was. I'd come back and see her and we'd sit on the swings and we'd kiss under the slide. I was going to miss her.

The main entrance to the big comprehensive school had a series of brick banks. Think Barbican in London. Grey, oppressive and a bit science fiction with a Maggie Thatcher budget. There was a shortcut that took you in a straight line avoiding the steps. The only thing was, you had to slide down the bank. It was basically an extended skid, but with my slippery school shoes and a good run up, I could slide the whole way down and keep sliding for at least another three feet, which is exactly where I bumped into my girlfriend from the year below.

"Park?" Question and location.

"'Kay." French smile.

"Bye!" Sharp exit.

By the time I said "Bye!", I was three feet away, so I just carried on. I ran away quite fast in my slippery shoes and my leg jiggled for the rest of the day while I tried to imagine the coolest way to let her know I was leaving town and that I would never see her again. It was probably best to imagine I'd been killed in some kind of action situation saving a cat. Most of the time we'd walk there together. I'd take her bag and tell her it wasn't heavy and throw mine in the bushes to prove that I wasn't bound by rules. Kids hate rules. In fact, it's rule number one. Rule number two on the other hand is, 'Don't fight gangs on your own'. When I saw the look of defiance in her eyes as she sat under the slide surrounded by five boys banging five sticks, I thought that's definitely a gang.

I was late, just for effect. The effect being, pretending I wasn't nervous. I didn't want to tell her we probably had to break up and I was leaving tomorrow. My reality was that I never went back, so what was the point. No mobile phones, no pagers, no texts, no emails no Facebook. An address written on a Kit-Kat wrapper was the best you could expect, but what kind of teenager likes writing letters? When they span around to glare, I decided I'd tell her later. It had been a while since I had seen the big boy face-to-face. Being the year below we only passed each other in corridors, usually accompanied by an insult relating to my mixed heritage and one relating to his massive fat head. Observing rule two, I asked the damsel in distress if she was alright and tried to ignore the pole wielding boys. She nodded. The five boys closed in, bunching together to stop me from seeing her.

"You might as well say bye to her now!" A threat.

That was kind of the plan you dick head.

I pushed past them and stopped in front of Joanne, the five boys behind me. One of them shouted, "Get her bag!" Grabby hands.

Now wait a minute. She was my girlfriend, that bag was my responsibility. Without moving towards or away from the hustle, I firmly gripped the sloping sides of the slide roof creating a teenage barrier of half-Chinese arms. I could feel the weight of them behind me trying to bend my arms the wrong way. No problem, I had a sweet grip and they were pushing my arms into the slide, which only made my barrier stronger. They should have pulled my hands away, idiots. Crack. It was like being hit on the arms with a three-foot-stick. Which is exactly what happened. The first one took me by surprise. It hurt. Within the space of about ten seconds they'd all had a go. My arms were taking a beating but I would never let go. Joanne looked scared. Sat neatly under the slide with her pretty French face she winced each time they struck me. Crack, wince, glare. Crack, wince, hang on. Crack, wince, easy. It sounded like a laugh. Maybe my homemade video based Kung Fu training was complete. I think it unnerved them. The pain had changed to some kind of strange excitement. I could see that the sticks were giving way. Some of them were just bamboo, some of them were rotten. They started to snap. The five boys were as useless as their weapons.

"Is that all you got?" I had at least six more hits in my arm.

I laughed again, Joanne looked up. I'd like to say I winked at her, but I think it was a grimace as the last homemade weapon faltered and broke in two on my reddening outstretched arms. I didn't turn around as they left. I locked my arms up on the slide and looked at Joanne to gauge where they were. When I could tell that they were finally far enough away, I sat down. I could hear them shouting that I was dead, I needed to watch my back, just you wait and promises of stronger sticks, maybe even nails. Joanne asked me why I wasn't scared. At the perfect moment to tell her the reason I wasn't scared of a revenge attack was because I was leaving town, she kissed me on the lips and I forgot how to talk.

4.

For the next couple of years, I got my action fix from my skateboard and my girl fix from home economics class. It was great. Nearly the whole of every Tuesday was made up of me and my buddy Jeff and twenty-eight girls with bags full of food. Occasionally we were allowed to sit outside under a tree. Me and Jeff getting free snacks and relaxing in the sun. They kept talking about exams and big life decisions, but how can you think about that kind of thing when the scones are so fresh and the breeze is just enough for me and Jeff to steal a glimpse of scandalous elastic. Heaven.

It was the first day after spring half term when I first spoke to her, I just thought she was Irish. To be sure I asked my buddy Jonathan. Dude. I'd lived in Ireland, it was an instant connection. She had long curly wild brown hair and the figure of a gymnast, she was shy and knowing and she had secrets. Secrets I wanted to know about, secrets that my friends said I shouldn't get too concerned with. Trying to get time with this girl alone was hard.

"I can never come to your house." Final.

No worries, I have a skateboard and a BMX.

"And you can never come to mine." Double final. And that's that. Parents. Strict much.

I thought that was harsh. When I dug a little deeper she'd said that people like her can't mix with people like me. It was a strange revelation, because even though it was me sat there with the face of two races, it was herself she was referring to as the outsider. I was hooked. What the fuck was her secret?

I had cleverly engineered a trip out of town with my sultry Irish friend. A group of us were offered a free trip to Skegness. A funky youth worker at a local youth club had said we'd love it, we could even smoke fags, but don't tell anyone. All we had to do was turn up at the car park. It was vaguely to do with charity, so I think that must have eased her parents' worries of their daughter being led astray by the devils on the dunes. One of us had swiped some booze and cleverly concealed it in a Tango bottle, but sitting squashed next to my gaelic charm in a full coach of day trippers that were more at home licking the window than looking out of it, we changed our minds. At first we took the piss. We laughed. We couldn't help it. Janet had showed me her lunch box at least two hundred times and we'd only been driving for twenty minutes. The lady who organised the trip was a good woman, genuinely cool, and because of her we started to play nice. Our clever jokes were wasted on them anyway. They were just pleased to be hurtling down the road on the way to see the sea, and they were happy. We sang along with the radio. Their jokes were crazy, but so were they. They laughed, and we laughed with them.

Trying to light a BBQ on a windy sand dune is hard enough, but with the funky youth worker insisting that we all stop breathing to help the flames it becomes a nightmare. I wanted to punch him in the face for being annoying but I was behaving myself. After a round of sand garnished, almost cooked burgers, the day finally put its feet up. Some of the boys were playing football with the guys that were able, and some of the girls were just sitting watching the waves with the guys who preferred to sit down. I had two hours until we had to leave, a secretive Irish beauty and a mile of sand dunes. I took her hand and we went to explore.

After a round of death defying leaps into the soft dry sand I was hot. No sauce yet. I was just hot. Wearing her black one-piece swimsuit all she had to do was take off her shorts and she was ready for a dip. I've never been a fan of deep water but I never liked being sweaty. I stood up to my waist and watched as she splashed about and went under the water. The melt of a scorching summer day mixed with the freezing cold North Sea must have done something to her. Grabbing my hand, she led me back up to the sand dunes. We crashed to the floor, her hair wet and her breath deep and we kissed. French kissed. She wasn't shy anymore. Her beach wear saved her modesty but my hands were having all the fun of the fair. Keen to check me for any cuts or scratches I may have procured during my beach stunts her hands were also exploring adventurously. It was magnificent. Bonjour Madame, je voudrais une packet de bon bons sil vous plait.

A few days later we were walking through town together after school. I'd managed to get her to hold my hand finally. She'd been so scared before of being seen with me in public, but after our half hour in the sand things were getting serious. They called us 'gorgers'. If you weren't a gypsy traveller that's what you were. While they lived free off the land and worked their charms on the locals, they looked down on the rest of the world and didn't steal or fight one bit. She was embarrassed to explain at first.

"I can't get wit ya cuz yous is a gorgers." Irish accent.

"So, you think I'm gorgeous do you?" High maturity level.

Before I could even get a laugh, a bright yellow transit van skidded to a halt on the pedestrian crossing. Shit! It was her uncle. His name was Bodge. He wasn't very keen on his niece mixing with the local people, no matter how 'Gorgeous' I was, especially not a half-Chinese one. He leaned across to the passenger side, opened the door and said,

"GET IN THE FUCKIN CAAAAAAH!" Transit anger.

Instantly my hand was empty. She didn't even look back at me as she obeyed and climbed head-down into the van. Bodge shot me a stare that said it all and with crunching gears and a burst of black smoke, they were gone. The next day at school, people wondered where she was. The next week at school, people thought she'd been kidnapped. The next month at school, it was like she'd never even been there. Traveller kids came and went according to my friends. Not because they moved, but when the girls got old enough they were married off and filled with babies. Dangerous liaisons. There were rumours that the other boys on the site would beat her for stooping so low, for daring to insult the centuries old traditions of the travelling community. I thought they were all full of shit – I saw nothing honourable in driving around in

Ford transit vans stealing scrap and fighting the locals. It was strange. I realised that my romantic adventures had a wider effect than the one on my teenage heart. I felt bad. I was warned not to go looking for her and with stories of men having their hands cut off and people getting buried in fields, I decided I probably wouldn't.

5.

My brother wasn't old enough to be left alone at home. Often I'd babysit. We'd play with Lego and make spaceships and I'd cook him dinner while our Mum and Dad were at work. My mate Jim would drive around and we'd smoke joints in the garden when my brother finally went to bed. It was fun. I knew that evening I would be on little bro duties, so I decided to rent a couple of videos from the Blockbuster's around the corner. I couldn't choose between Mutant Turtles or Care Bears. I knew he loved both, but which one did I want to sit through for the 200th time?

She scoffed at the sight of me on the floor, brow furrowed, in turmoil. Magic teddies or radical mutants? I turned around to see who was judging me so harshly and I was instantly confused, then smitten. I'd been living in this town for a couple of years now. Unnaturally settled. I knew all the mildly ethnic people and they knew me. This girl was obviously half-something, almost certainly yellow. Where was my memo? Cheek bones that could cut mangoes and a public school edge that made me feel inferior as I sat on the floor holding cartoons. I managed a chuckle, she threw me a flirty smile and before I could stand up she was gone. I asked around. Who was this half-oriental beauty and how come I'd never heard about her before? No one seemed to know what I was talking about.

"Oh, so this half-Chinese babe gave you the eye and now she's vanished? Chinny Reck On.

"Fuck off! She's real! I saw her in Blockbusters!" Defiant.

"Yeah, yeah get back to your magic rabbits and make your bro some noodles you twat." Hmm.

For the next couple of days, I hung around the market place on my skateboard outside Blockbuster. Nothing. Not a peep. I had no idea who she was, where she lived or who her friends were and I was starting to think I'd imagined the whole thing. How could there be a mixed race girl so beautiful living in the same town as me and know nothing about her. Thursday rolled around and I was starting to lose faith. Maybe I did imagine her after all.

A few weeks before, our little skateboard gang had been interviewed about a ramp that we were trying to build. We'd raised a few hundred pounds from the council, from the Prince's Trust and we had a five quid donation from Marks & Spencer. My friend Jonny had phoned the takeaway to tell me that there was a little article about our half-pipe dream in the local paper. I scrambled excitedly through the pages looking for our fifteen lines of fame and there she was. A full page spread about a local girl who had won a major modelling contract with a top agency in London, she'd been crowned the 'Face of '93'. Her life was about to change fast. I needed to get in there before she moved away.

The article explained everything. She was half-Malaysian and her parents owned a pub in town. Her

education was paid for and her friends loved 'Ruggers'
– she was a high class babe and I didn't mind being the
tramp to her lady. Armed with the information for love I
headed straight over to the pub and waited until I casually
'bumped' into her once more.

Her parents had sent her to a posh school, at least
posh for me, which is why she didn't hang out much in
town. She played badminton and worked part-time at a
restaurant out of the area. I told her that I'd meet her after
work.

"But you don't even have a car?" True. "Just be there
after work!" Success.

I was so excited. Not only had I managed to bag a
model, but I'd never really kissed a girl who wasn't white.
I was full of myself and scared in equal measures. What
strange exotic delights awaited me?

Waiting in the car park for her we played our latest
rave mixtape as loud as possible. It was the glory days of
new electronic repetitive beats and ecstasy and we used
any excuse to dance. I'd drawn our 'Boom Crew' ravers
gang logo on my friend Chris' red all in one boiler suit,
and he'd driven us there so he could show everybody his
dance moves and his couture dance fashion. It was great,
she loved my artistic handiwork. She thought we were
cute doing our hardcore shuffle in the car park. She was
more into funky jazz but it didn't matter. Chris was my
weekend wing man and he was impressed. This girl was
stunning and I was going to go around to see her while her
parents were working at the pub. A few days before I was
on ecstasy. Now I was in it.

Our first taste of sauce together was strange. I was mainly worried about being caught by her parents and getting splattered. She was very animated. Even with the Brand New Heavies muffling the thumps I was scared that her Dad would come running up as she wailed and twisted, but she stopped moaning at the exact time I popped my condiment. Great! What teenage synchronicity. We were perfectly aligned. I think she almost fainted under the sheer power of my sexual Kung Fu and as we hugged goodbye I felt like a boss.

LSD is a funny drug. The slightest thing can turn a good trip in to a nightmare. It could be stepping on a spider that you have just talked to, it could be realising that you've been sick in a builder's helmet and should have told someone before they tried it on. Or, it could be your girlfriend phoning you at a house party and telling you she faked an orgasm. I really had no idea why she wanted to be so honest. Part of me appreciated the call but only seconds earlier I had been quite happy watching my friend Steve try and work out if the cats on the wall were three dimensional or just gravy stains. As I put the phone down I didn't know what to say. It had taken quite a lot of effort to not eat the phone so when someone asked me what the call was about I just replied.

"Erm, apparently she faked it." Thoughtful.

"Faked what?" Wobbly face.

"Faked your cat bananarama." Going.

"Hey Swany's got a banana phone!" Going.

"Why is this phone trying to knit my cat gloves ..." Gone.

I remembered what she'd said on the phone a couple of minutes before I met her for lunch in Brown's in Nottingham. I was going to meet her friends for the first time. I was nervous. I like to think I can make a good impression at the best of times but her honest admission had thrown me for a weird one. I wondered if she'd told her little circle, would they be laughing at my naivety. As I walked out of the little bar a few minutes later, it wasn't only my naivety they'd been laughing at. No. It was my clothes, my taste in music, my Walkman, my parents and my hair.

I was a raver and proud. I felt like I was part of a secret club and we had the answers to a better way of life. We just wanted to share the peace love and unity through stacks of speakers and Technic 1210s. All of my friends were DJs and MCs. We put on illegal parties. They'd play records, I'd grab the mic. Some of us sold drugs and some of us danced until sunrise, it was ours and we loved it.

The assortment of public school boys sat around the table didn't love it. It turns out they thought the whole thing was pointless. They couldn't imagine dancing in a field in the middle of the night. They thought drugs were for losers, prostitutes, and the poor. With my hand outstretched ready to engage with firmness I was thrown when the first words weren't "Hello", but rather,

"Where do you winter?"

Make it good. "Somewhere warm innit mate!" Make 'em laugh.

"Drive?"

Make it a turbo. "Skateboard!" I'm rad.

"School?" League tables.

"Is bollocks!" Rebel without the sauce. And without a laugh.

As far as I was concerned, I'd never been proud of my education. I'd never had to be. School was for laughing and kissing not for being pleased about. Who were these idiots? The idiots were her peers and her peers seemed to be all peering at me. Peering at my shaved head with a foot-long dreadlock, and my huge massive baggy purple raving trousers. They didn't seem to want to share any peace or love, let alone unity, at all. My girlfriend laughed along with them; poor little me, comprehensive and state educated. I felt like a complete knob.

I passed my driving test after a handful of lessons and was given the keys to the takeaway delivery car. As long as I got it back before opening the roads belonged to me. I was excited to be able to drive to Nottingham and meet her. We were going to have a walk through the arboretum. I didn't know what that was but I was sure I'd work it out once I got there, something about trees. Being a first time driver I was careful. I was super careful. I was checking my rearview mirror. I was checking my rearview mirror so intently that when I finally glanced back at the road in front of me, I was moments away from a collision. The white Lada in front of me had slammed on its brakes. I panicked and slammed on my brakes. Skidding towards the stationary car I had three options. Veer right into the oncoming traffic. Nope. Veer left into the unplugged field. Nope. Hold tight and close your eyes as the car in fro...BANG! My first crash. The metallic zing that had shot through my body on impact left my heart racing. No one was hurt. The reason that the car had stopped suddenly was because of the driver's daughter. The front of my Rover Kensington was gone. Crumpled and pathetic. The only damage to the car in front was an almost invisible scratch. An invisible scratch right next to the disabled sticker. I'd done it again. The driver's daughter had been having some kind of fit and in the panic he'd done the natural thing and stopped the car so he could help her. I should have been looking. It wasn't funny.

I didn't get to meet her in the trees and a couple of weeks later she wanted to 'talk'. Letting me down gently she said that we were from different worlds, and the truth of it was that we were. She was moving to London soon to start her modelling career so it was probably for the best. I saw the logic in this. After all, London was a hundred miles away and I'd just crashed my car. Logic however wasn't an issue when my mate Barry John drove me to her auntie's house just so I could scream at her. I'd discovered that the whole time she was only on a break with some rugby fella. I was some kind of subversive culture holiday. As we drove back home with our rave tapes blasting in BJ's beige Allegro, I thought to myself I don't need this ego bashing. I was an MC, we did parties in hidden quarries, we stomped our feet until tractors threatened to run us over. I was better than this. I didn't care that she was a model. I made a vow that the next girl I fell for would be a bonafide four to the floor hardcore pill popping love child, but by the time summer had rolled around again I was starting to think that the chances of that happening in a small market town in the middle of nowhere were slim.

6.

Breaking and entering is illegal. The law was not for us. We were so far underground not even a loosely tied rope could stop us. Dropping LSD in the afternoon was magical. It meant that it wasn't just the lights and echoes of the night that provided the pyrotechnics and laughter. Sitting on the Broadmarsh banks watching the little kids skateboarding through the shoppers, she put a pigeon feather in my single plaited dreadlock. One of the boys asked if we were hippies. She smiled and said yes, and we eat pigeons. Techno hippies would have been more fitting, but they were eleven years old.

We wandered around the city chewing sunglasses, following smoke trails and hiding our giggles until it was night. Time flies when you're flying. In a blink we were standing in front of a boarded up carousel in the centre of the city. A loosely tied rope, our only barrier into an unknown realm of firetrucks and one-seat jumbo jets. We had to get in. The street lights shone just bright enough through the thin tarpaulin. The world outside forgot it existed. Everything glittered. The diamond shaped bulbs that lined every surface were singing to us. We crammed our bums into any seat that could take it and we became rulers of the secret fun fair, the King and Queen of the merry-go-round. We knew we couldn't stay forever. Surely, someone would be coming soon to evict us and put an end to our acid adventure so we decided to escape. Summoning the courage to leave and saying goodbye to our favourite funny cars we ran out, tarpaulin flapping behind us. We both stopped dead. We were trapped in a beam of light.

All I could see was her. Her scruffy dungarees, her wild spaced out eyes, her chunky boots and her explosion of curly blonde hair. She was looking up into the beam of light, she saw something. A single point moving in slow motion.

"Snowflake!" Its June.

"I can see it!" It's real!

At the same time, we shouted. "IT'S SNOWING!" Synchronicity.

As we watched the single snowflake drift slowly to the floor in front of us, all that was left in the universe was me and her. This girl was four to the floor hardcore. She made it snow in summer and I wanted to be with her for the rest of my life.

For a short while we lived in a strange drug-fuelled bliss. No one had jobs. We treated the dole office like a fortnightly battle against 'the man', only it was a battle that we left each time with a prize of £74.68. We were winners. We drove around country lanes in the middle of the night searching for phone boxes that would lead us to hidden rave arenas and when we got there we danced until it was a different day. Life was fast. Life was about lasers and ecstasy, nothing could stop us. We had the keys to a brave new world. We were invincible.

Being invincible meant nothing could touch us. Not a

thing. When I dropped the little sheet of acid on a Tuesday afternoon by myself, I watched the floor tilt slightly. I instantly felt 'vincible'. I was about to have my first and last bad trip. My raving techno hippie girlfriend became my knight in shining armour. Grabbing me with our friend Kate, she forced me into her little car and they drove me to a huge open field. Nowhere to hurt myself, nothing to jump off, just grass, air, and fear. She stayed with me for hours, making sure I was okay. When I could finally make sense of the world and speak English, she took me to her house, wrapped me up in blankets and I slept. I slept the sleep of a man who had just seen all his friends' eyes melt and the sky turn into a giant Eagle and flap the solar system away with a massive swish. She knew everything. She made me feel safe.

When the film Trainspotting came out we all laughed at its bleakness, we knew better. Drugs were great and they never hurt anyone right? Wednesday rolled around and the weekend begun again. Having decided to take a break from LSD, my ginger DJ buddy and I had spent a few days trying out drinks. We wanted a perfect summer soother. Sitting in our garden we'd finally decided on peach schnapps. Fruity and sophisticated, the obvious choice for a bunch of unemployed ravers. Sat in our garden, pleased that we'd finally found our summer spritzer, I downed a pint of our newfound favourite beverage. Wednesday was the night to pull the 'Greebo' chicks at the local sticky night club. I darted back into the house to get ready. Tonight was gunna be mental!

The sound was intense. The pain was incredible. I'd

severely misjudged how you open a door. I'd imagined that as I leapt, my outstretched hand would pop open the door and my momentum would carry me through with tones of Fred Astaire. Luckily our housemate Brian had just arrived and his car was running. He'd arrived at the precise time that I'd run face-first through a plate glass door. I owe him my life. It was bad. I lost four pints of blood and almost lost an eye. After hours of emergency surgery to first stop the bleeding and then patch me up, I was eventually wheeled into my ward. I couldn't smile, open my mouth or eat. I'd lacerated my lips in the mess. Someone needed to stay with me. The stitches were good, but I was still bleeding.

Through the haze of morphine and adrenalin I heard her voice. She was with Kate, they'd driven to see me, they wanted to help. I heard her clumpy dance boots before I saw her. I could tell by the look in her eyes it was bad. The doctors wanted me to have a therapy session before they let me see the damage. This time I slept like a man that had almost killed himself jumping through a glass door, but when I woke there she was. Surrounded by bloodied tissues and empty tea cups, she'd stayed by my side all night tending to my wounds as I dreamt the dream of a stupid boy.

They say a flame that burns twice as bright burns half as long, but this girl was a grenade. She needed to explode. When she told me she was leaving she handed me a letter. The world was out there and she had to see it. A few weeks later I was feeling sad, I didn't want to her leave. I needed her. The thought of her leaving made me feel sick, angry confused, stupid. I agonised about the day she was leaving but more about the day after when she'd be too far away to save me. I had to see her. I skateboarded to her house, it was late. I let myself in and after a quick toke with my buddies I ventured up to her room. All I wanted to do was curl up next to her and cuddle. I was surprised to find him in her bed, but we were ravers and we shared a lot of peace and love and unity, and occasionally that meant crashing in a bed with ten other people. As I started to climb in bed next to her, he said,

"We're kind of busy mate." Hiding his boner.

"That's cool, I just want a cuddle." It was hidden well.

"No. Busy. Busy…" She threw the grenade at my chest.

I hadn't even realised that something was going on between them. It was a complete curveball, especially as I'd always thought he was a bit of a twat. I felt like the biggest idiot in the room. Which I was. No cuddles for me tonight. Two weeks later I was crying into my pillow, and she was serving drinks in a bar in Denmark.

7.

I was living my life like a comet. Hurtling through the blackness like a shiny ball with gas coming out of my arse, only narrowly avoiding crashing headfirst into a planet. That's how I wanted it. I'd escaped death by door and I was lucky to be alive. The girl of my dreams was pulling pints in Denmark and more than likely pulling the Danes that wanted them. I was lost. I put my thoughts down to try and stop the sadness creeping in. I wrote rap songs. I collaborated with a local musician called Pete and we wrote a song called 'Soul Kissing' – it was pretty good. I was a heart- broken-cheesy-drug-addict-rave-MC who wanted to be a pop star. I decided that flying solo for a while could be good. Get my head down, make the connections. Life was more important than girls, kissing and even love. All love did was fuck you up. I became as jaded as my lucky rabbit. I scoffed at couples. I squeezed my sauce at every pretty girl that had chips to offer and I was greedy. My attitude towards life was Eat Me. Fuck you. I was Bart Simpson. Hell yeah. Loose-mouthed, skateboarder, short and yellow. I was in a gang. A troupe of baseline junkies. We'd strut around town off our faces on anything we could swallow, snort or steal. We'd steal spray paint and tag car parks, road signs. Anywhere we liked. It was mostly quite decorative, some of the crew had real talent. We were proud of our neon vandalism.

I knew that there was something at the end of the old-fashioned narrow arcade. It was a busy Saturday afternoon so my view was blocked. I'd just have to wait until I was right in front of it. Huge orange letters. Two words. Eat and Me. I was pretty stoked. Oh yes. Fuck the rules, fuck telling me where I can paint words and … fuck me, who was that?

The young man holding her hand had only allowed me one single frame of existence. It must have been a strong grip. A secret grip of a young man who knows he is about to lose something incredible. I had stolen one single frame of existence and that was all I needed. In that one frame I saw the most beautiful smile I had ever seen. It was as if every single cell in her body was beaming. That single frame was a stolen moment. In that moment she told me her whole life story, what she loved, what she hated, who she wanted to be and that she would fall in love with me the instant I found her again. That single stolen frame of existence was all I needed to be one hundred percent certain that this girl would one day be my wife.

• • •

It was the perfect summer. Nothing less. By now our little dance collective were well connected, mobile and inked up. There were three cars full that evening. All I knew was that it was in a barn. We were all well versed in finding illegal parties but looking out for lasers and a thousand people was easier than a little eighteenth birthday party in someone's uncle's shed. We'd been driving for a couple of hours. No one had any idea where the party was. I couldn't even ring anyone. We all had pagers. Pagers were cool, but ultimately rubbish. I knew our convoy was getting tired of each new dead end. Our gravelly turning circle getting less patient each time as we turned tail into another B-road. One more, I promise. One more. Success.

Our arrival had caused concern. Who and why are these raver types here? They'll steal the new CD player for acid powders. How did they change the music? That's very, very loud! It was a perfect diversion. Every male who had eyes and could walk would have been crowding around her normally. She was newly single. The young man who had pulled her away from me in that sunny arcade had lost his grip forever.

"You are the most beautiful thing I have ever seen in my life." I had to tell her.

"So are you." Champagne super nova.

I couldn't believe it. I'd been a fan of cool magazines like Sky and Empire and Just Seventeen. I was a secret fan boy. I loved the glossy pictures. I loved beautiful celebrities, it fascinated me. I knew who was hot and who was not. I could name every super model in George Michael's classic video for 'Too Funky' and I'd pulled a few models myself by now. I had a fair idea that my new girlfriend was simply the most beautiful woman to have ever been born. On top of that, she was funny. She hardly wore make up, just Vaseline on her lips. Her face was perfect. All I ever wanted to do was see her smile, and when she laughed it made me feel like I was the cleverest, funniest, coolest most perfect man that had ever been born.

The only thing I saw in her face when she screamed at me was hatred. She was my mirror. So much anger between two people who a thousand days ago were drunk with love. I loved how people adored her. I loved how people told me it was perfect, but the blame in her eyes made every one of my nine lives choke, and afterwards, I hated how people told me I was stupid. The doctor had told her there were complications.

I'd never known anyone who could make me so angry. I knew I loved her. The feelings I had for her scared me. It was bigger than I could cope with. All my life I'd considered myself a romantic, a player, but now half the time I didn't even know what game it was. Should I roll the dice or run between her legs? I didn't even know what happened when you lost but there were so many times I wished I could have started again. My life was an equal fill of heaven and hell. One minute kissing behind DJ booths in nightclubs, and the next throwing hateful insults across the Paris metro as she ran in tears into an echoey foreign maze. We'd been together for longer than I'd known most of my friends put together. It was surreal. I knew her family. We'd buy each other's pets presents, it was my first real relationship. When she told me she loved me I believed her. When I told her I loved her I meant it. What I did now was important. Things were getting serious.

My best friend Jonny and old housemate Dennis had bought a little wine bar. It was the coolest place in town. The Nineties were coming to an end and we were making heaps of money shifting cheap slush puppy cocktails to underage drinkers. I'd been given the keys. It was a success.

We had the perfect blend of staff and punters and the music was banging. We even had a gypsy on the door. He once held me over the balcony by my ankle and laughed promising, "I won't drop ya little fella!" No, please don't.

Dangling aside, he was great at getting everyone to fuck off if I wanted to go home before 2AM. I'd dance with the love of my life behind the bar when our latest favourite song came on. She'd work with me at weekends. We'd spend the afternoons shopping for outfits to wear that evening. We had to dress to impress. I felt like a rockstar when I walked in with her. The crowds would cheer when we all boogied, we'd give free shots to our mates and everything was perfect.

I was used to leaving friends behind. All my life I'd had to let go quickly, even if we had the most fun ever, make sure you hug them, and wave with all your heart. A big wave until you can't see their eyes anymore. The last thing they see is a big smile and a wave. What could be better than that?

My beautiful girlfriend was away with her Dad, broken families equals the occasional weekend obligatory. Standing in a phone booth near her Mum's house I told her my friend Richard had died. The cold silver phone box and the faint smell of piss my only companion as I delivered the worst news yet. She told me she was coming back to get me. All I wanted to do was be with her. Life slowed down. We argued because me and Brent wanted to drive to the funeral in the back of an open top BMW. The three of us had a little electro band called 'Formidable Force' and we'd recorded a couple of tracks. It was looking good, of course, until we lost a genius. Richard was in funky house heaven and Brent went to New York and never came back, lured away with cute accents, cute butts and the sunshine of the States. All of a sudden, I needed her more than life itself.

We argued about everything. We explored. We argued. We changed. We promised. We wandered. We fought. I hated her. She hated me. I loved her so much. She loved me so much. She wanted to leave. I had to go. We both knew it was ending. I got angry instead of scared. She got bitchy instead of worried. I wanted a blonde with big tits. She changed her pill. She wanted an Uzi for my stoner cocky bollocks. We pushed on through. We tried to save it. She changed her pill. We had final desperate sex. She changed her pill. I said I didn't mind waiting. She said she didn't care. We added a little sauce to the dish. She got pregnant. We only found out four months later when our unborn baby was dead and trapped inside her pipes.

I noticed that she had a little bump. I was used to seeing her naked, we'd have fun trying on outfits and doing fashion shows. It was good clean kinky fun, we wanted to kill each other, but often that fire would bring us back together. We were drinking a lot of free cocktails and eating takeaway food and I'd known the strength of her ringed fist if I upset her so I decided not to bring it up. Besides, the leopard skin thigh high boots, black G-string and submachine gun she was posing with were a more interesting focal point if I was to critique her openly.

We both knew it was risky. We'd argued for hours, back and forth endless accusations, paranoia, blame,

blame, blame. I was leaving town for university. I was twenty-four years old. I had dreams. I wanted fame and fortune and being stuck in the Midlands with the world's most beautiful young woman just wasn't enough. She wanted more, the world was calling her. I wasn't enough with my weed addiction and my fucking skateboard. I got so pissed off when I realised she deserved so much more. I took my boots to her little blue car like a clockwork orange. I wanted to smash it to bits and cut my wrists with the splinters. I didn't care how embarrassed she'd be when she had to tell her Dad that her stupid boyfriend had kicked the shit out of her little blue Nova. How dare the universe better me. Why was it taking her away? I didn't hate her; I was angry that she was strong enough to let it end. She'd seen the devil inside of me and had risen above my snarling passion. I was a beast. I wanted to hurt her, make everyone see how evil she was. I embarrassed her. I screamed at her from car windows until my throat burned and my eyes stung with rage. I did hurt her, and everyone saw how evil I was. We tried to be civil. We had to respect the years and the losses. I felt as if I had stopped the most beautiful girl I had ever seen from becoming real. We'd talked about babies and how cute they'd be. It would be a crime if our genes didn't mix. We'd talked about babies and how she'll never have them. It felt like a crime to me.

Managing the busiest cocktail bar in town with your stunning girlfriend was a blast, everyone wanted her, I had the biggest cock in the room. News travels fast in small towns. Everyone wanted her but now I was the biggest cock in the room. They looked like packs of dogs crowding around her, finally allowed to impress and steal her away. I couldn't handle it. I'd have to encourage rugby team boys to knock back half pints of tequila, they'd lift me up over the bar and cheer. Moments later I'd have to run into the little brick kitchen as my whole life was ripped out of my chest and I'd just cry when I saw her happy with everyone else but me. I had to fire her. It wasn't pretty. All that I had left to do was kick her dog Mollie in the balls and my work would be done.

Sitting in her garden. Her Mum was out, sister playing hockey. Wearing all black. A funeral. I hadn't seen her this calm in months. I'd forgotten how to look at her. I'd just seen a version of myself. Angry, bitter. I knew it was over, she wouldn't look at me. Careful. Every move neutral. Her stillness made me regret every moment of madness. It was quiet.

I'd been getting rid of my things in the little bedsit I was living in. Throwing away plates and saucepans. Getting rid of the rubbish. A clean start. A new town. Of all the times I wished I could have started again, now was that time and I felt new. We were heading in opposite directions. North and South in almost a perfect line. There had to be a final goodbye. We had spent enough time together to witness each other's journey, it had to mean something. In her garden we talked. There were things I had to understand. Things I had to remember. The doctors had told her there were complications. I knew this. She broke down into tears when she told me that she couldn't have children. This was complicated. It was my fault. It was so complicated, the only thing I could remember was that it was my fault. That was easier. She would never be a mother. I had broken her. Was perfect, now fucked. Easy. Not complicated at all. At twenty-four years old I left to get my degree. I'd been mucking around for too long now. It was my fault. Out of sight, out of mind. I wanted the distance to be a million miles. I wanted to shoot myself in the brain. My blood turned to acid and my sleep was a hurricane of sweat and bloodied knuckles. I wanted to just kiss her one last time. I knew if I kissed her, she'd forget everything and like magic everything I broke would be fixed.

Sitting in her garden. Her Mum was out, her sister playing hockey. I knew it was over for good this time. I asked her for one last kiss goodbye and she said "no". She said "no" to all of my most treasured ways. Everything she had ever liked about me I tried to be, all at once and all too late. She kept saying "no" and looked down at the big cup of cold tea. My longest and most important relationship had ended. It was the first time in my life I wished I wasn't leaving, but even if I'd stayed, she wouldn't be there. I knew it was over when she refused my magic kiss. People change. Dreams change. Life goes on and tea gets cold.

8.

I sat in the row opposite her in my first cinema lecture. I loved it. I loved being at university. I was older than most of the other students and Jan, my partner in crime, shared my love of movies, shared my age and my love of vintage leather jackets. We were like 'Donnie Brasco' and 'Tyler Durden', if you squinted hard enough and had never seen a film before. We were watching the opening to Top Gun but with the music from Silence of the Lambs. It blew my mind. Speed garage was the latest thing and I loved that too. The urban styles of the young women made everywhere look like a cheap hip hop video. I loved that even more. Malaysian. How strange. This time she was full Malay and full Muslim. I never asked if it was something to do with her religion, but she always said that even though she really wanted to, she could never take my willy out for a picnic with her face. If you know what I mean. This struck me as odd. Not that I'd ever force any kind of mouth picnic on anyone. Allah certainly didn't stop her from carrying a rock of uncut cocaine around with her in a little silver mirror case. University was excellent. I was learning all about culture, watching films in class and learning about religion. It was amazing.

I was a student, I knew shit. Every news item had some kind of Millennium Bug. Planes were going to vaporise into phone boxes and all the hairdryers would explode.

Crock of shit. Nothing was going to happen. I only held my breath at the stroke of midnight in case there was some kind of apocalypse alarm, but nothing rang. No gong, no bells, no chimes. Just a coked up Malaysian Muslim giving my friend Jay a lap dance as he smiled, eyes rolling back from six quid tablets. Happy new year.

I'd been trying to move for nearly two hours. Frozen solid with my last bump of ketamine I knew I had to do something. Something annoying.

"Your bewer's fuckin' radged chavvy!" Newark slang.

I had to get her out of the house. My pocket-sized urbanette had decided to shoot a bold claim. Soap opera accusations based on me having shared life and death with the people around us and her, who couldn't even remember their names. All I could do was run away. I had to take control of the situation, this was too much hassle. Everything about her was a pain in the arse.

Christmas is, and always will be a special time for me. I like it because you can look forward to it together, as a couple, as a country, as a planet. It always comes in winter and there's a special time my brother and I call 'The Invisible Week', where no one knows what to do. Eat chocolates in your dressing gown, read magazines in the toilet and stay up late. Ho, ho, ho. Having a girlfriend at this time of year can cause problems logistically. Especially if they want to spend time with me and their own family. So, I did what I normally did and said,

"Come for Christmas at my Mum's house, it will be Christmassy as fuck." Seasonal enticement and a lot of festive judgement.

I'd once read the whole of Matilda in one sitting, so long loo breaks were nothing new to me or my family. I'd expected at best a jab about being lighter but as I sat down I noticed that my festive guest was furious. My Stepdad almost nodding off, my Mum in dressing gown with cat on lap and fire glowing. My little brother playing video games.

"Why were you so long?" Loud.

"What? I been to the loo …" Oh it's a joke.

"You didn't tell me you were going to the loo!" Intricate humour structure maybe?

"What? I was? Are you …" Flustered.

"How dare you leave me by myself with these people!" Not funny.

"These people. Are you joking?" Not funny at all.

The biscuit tin haze was shattered with her brattish attitude. How dare I leave her? Really? How dare she think that a guest in a partner's house would be excused a completely unfounded outburst. Her insinuations that they weren't 'good' enough. She was judging everything. Not urban enough. Not Muslim enough. Sat in a country farm house with your half-Chinese boyfriend, his blonde white mother and her Northern farming husband watching TV shows about Jesus at Christmas, I'd have said not.

It wasn't quite a Danny Boyle dive but inside I felt like I belonged in a gutter. Windows closed, doors double locked. Chair up against it. Dance drug comedown. Soup and soft things. Bottles of sugary drinks and enough weed to get me to sleep. Curled up in a ball next to me was my film class girlfriend. Nose dripping, wheezing, sorry.

I was hiding away with embarrassment after the new year fiasco. It was nothing. Just twitchy bitchiness that mutated under the influence of powdered treats but added to the fact that she got mad when I had a poo, I was pretty sure this relationship was over. It was the start of the new millennium, the past was boring and my computer could still download porn. She told my Mum over our roast turkey dinner that she was looking forward to when I started thinking about becoming a Muslim. I spluttered a Yorkshire pudding. The look of confusion was the most interesting part. Mainly that she was confused why I hadn't thought about it seriously yet. This was a lot. We'd been together for a few months but there was no way I was going to start messing about with faith and all that kind of jazz. Surely we can all live in peace together? After all I had been born of the warehouse Nineties and I didn't care what colour you were, as long as you were the hottest girl in town. It was the start of a new millennium, surely we were all ready to move on from petty religious conflicts. Chinese, English, Muslim, Christians. All the same, right?

9.

The second year of a degree is where the chaff and wheat part ways. Some students come back after their first summer break with determined grit. The world is an oyster. You're a second year, sophisticated, you basically want all the shiny things. You crave a pearl. Some on the other hand have decided that they don't like shellfish and that pearls are just weird. By the time the Twin Towers had fallen, my Muslim girlfriend was no longer around. I'm not implying that she was involved or in any way extreme, but she had decided the world of edit suites, workshops and theatre wouldn't get her the life she wanted. I had no idea what she wanted. I knew that having sauce with her while she was on the phone to her friend should have been kinky. I knew at the very least it should feel a bit naughty. It wasn't. It was weird, cold. The sauce was stale. She was just chatting about an extra lecture she'd had and I was trying to listen in case I missed anything. I'd come to university to learn after all.

Second year meant I was out of halls and back in a house. I'd made good friends. The feeling of returning to something mid-stride made me feel great. For the first time in my life I felt grounded. I knew what to do, I knew where to go, I knew what to say, I knew what was expected of me, but I never expected the girl in the year above to be so hard to crack. My study buddy Benjy said I should come and see their new place. He'd moved in with seven other guys and they were going to try and play Halo together on their new superfast dial up. I didn't realise at the time but tucked away behind the maze of doorways and padlocks that lead me to gaming heaven, in a little one-bedroom flat was a girl that I'd spend the next seven years of my life with.

We were giggling and making really lame film jokes when she came in with a massive bag of doughnuts and said,

"You'll need these you fucking nerds." She told the truth.

There was a lull when she left. It was as if the air had turned back to arse biscuits and lynx. Eyes darting back and forth. Fuck it. Nerds.

"Who was that?" Where was my memo?

"Ah, she lives right behind us." Inside knowledge.

"Single?" Rabbit.

Foot gazing and shuffles can't be written effectively. I knew what was going on. They all fancied her and with their geographical advantage I needed to stake a bold claim. One I think must have been relayed and adopted as a challenge because as I got to know this girl, there was nothing that she couldn't do, and nothing that she'd give away until you absolutely, totally and utterly deserved it. Over the summer I'd worked at my old cocktail bar. Standing on the dance floor at 1.55 AM all I had to do was hold up a set of keys and utter two magic words and I'd take my pick of the scantily clad post booze delights. Lock. In. It was mostly hilarious and I had to get rid of the out of date booze anyway. They'd get a couple of bottles of slightly off Smirnoff Ice, and I'd get to live out my own private 'Hollyoaks – After Dark'. I was a heroic cartoon sleazebag with keys to a cocktail bar. To her, I was just some cocky student in the year below. She was studying theatre. I was studying film. She was already cooler than me. She had a magic power with her eyes. Over the years we discussed this power she had and I identified it to a minute shape change in her lids. It was subtle and hypnotic. She didn't need magic eyes. She was talented, driven and had exactly the same body shape as Kylie Minogue. I even measured her. Years later she had a body exactly the same size as Danni Minogue. Antipodean.

I made sure that I'd bump into her. She rolled with a little clique of young women. They reminded me of the film Heathers. That made me Christian Slater. The uni bar glitterati would whisk her away if the wrong kind of guys were chatting to her. I'd steal a bump and grind among the two steppers and MC Hammer lunatics with a thousand drunk students having the time of their lives falling around us. Each week I got a little closer. Each week she'd be pulled away by her team of taste makers. How dare she dally with the year below?

I'd been spending a lot of time with my Dutch housemate. We'd had some fun after I bumped into her at the Uni bar on a week night. She was dressed as a schoolgirl, beautiful honest blue eyes, Nordic blonde hair in pigtails and a lolly pop. Her Dad had a BAFTA and she made the best pancakes I've ever had. I wondered if I was falling in love with her. I wanted to tell her. She came home from Amsterdam and told me she was back with her boyfriend. I went over the road to see Benjy and have a man moan.

Empty house. Probably at the park getting pissed on Tesco cider. Fucking women. I called out. The back door was open and there she was. Putting out her washing in the little brick sun trap. The girl from the year above. She was wearing a thin hoodie and tiny denim short shorts and I could see all her tiny panties. I saw tea towels as well, but they're not as hot. At last I'd got her by herself. No clan of oestrogen to protect her, just G-strings blowing in the wind. I made knicker related small talk. I flashed my winning smile and turned my flirt on. She took the piss, told me to stay away from her undies and called me a pervert. I asked her why she liked those snooty girls and why she wasn't my girlfriend yet.

"I think they're little cunts and you haven't asked me out yet." Double facts.

Oh yeah. I hadn't actually asked her. The last time we were all hanging out together I just declared that I'd end up in bed with her. Bravado. I had nerd backup. My video game gang sniggered. What the hell? They doubt me? She laughed and threw a biscuit.

"No chance." Bring your best game.

I'd luckily escaped the Chinese curse. I wasn't a gambler but I bet her she'd be in bed with me before the end of term. I really shouldn't have been so cocky. I knew that the lads fancied her. Why wouldn't they? She was gorgeous, petite, creative. People would say she looked like a cross between Keira Knightly and Kylie. A whole lot of Ks.

I saw the play she wrote and directed for her final year. It made me cry. I was a budding film director and she had the stage. A perfect partnership. The Minogue arse and magic eyes, well that was just the icing on the cake. I became annoyed, we were wasting time. For god's sake woman, we need to fall in love right now.

I loved wearing beads. I'd been to Hong Kong and I'd picked up some chunky fat Buddha balls. I loved them. I never took them off. Ever. Not once. I took them off. I lost them. One night I heard a flap. Checking the hall way I found a note. Deciphering the cut out newspaper letters I realised the severity instantly. My beads had been stolen for ransom. There was a photo of my beads, dangling dangerously over a pile of rotten burgers. If I didn't come around at once, they would be finished. The address, a little one- bedroom flat behind a series of gates and padlocks.

I had to be impressed with her style. It was exactly the right thing to have sent me. I'd waited almost a year. Everyone knew I liked her. Her friends would whisk her away with a knowing look.

"You can't have her, fuck off second year." Beverly Hills 90210.

My heart was pounding as I stood in front of her door. Knock. Laughing. Candles. Mood lighting. Cool music. Everything clean and tidy. No one else. Wine and snacks. Complete Buffy VHS box set. Little bit more wine. Me and her. It was on.

It was getting late. Snacks untouched. Bottles empty. Ironic chick flick credits rolling with the sound down.

Worth the wait. I'd heard this all my life. I hated waiting for anything. I never understood why things didn't just happen at once. Instant gratification born of an Eighties childhood. We wanted it now because we were told the future would be hover boards and robot maids. It wasn't. I'd waited almost a year to bed this girl and it had to happen soon or…

"I'm gunna go…" Stop Talking.

"What, why?" Stay on target.

"Are we just gunna mess around or actually fu …" Shut your mouth.

She laughed and pulled me in. I melted onto her like cheese on toast. At last. We were going to explore each other's nakedness. I love being naked with girls. It's equally sexy and funny. It wasn't acrobatic. It wasn't noisy. It wasn't seedy. She wanted to know how it felt. How each touch and roll and embrace made me feel. It was poetic, it was sensual and it was perfect. I wanted to spend all my time with her. I needed to be by her side. We agreed that our bodies were friends. Let's do it. Let's get souls involved. Me and her against the world. A secret super team. I told her I was falling in love with her.

"I'm going to Africa." Shit, that's quite far.

It was only for a few months. No biggie. I was prepared to be in love with a whole planet between us. I had the keys to her flat and I moved in on flat sitting duties. My current housemates were pioneers of student stupidity and I loved them all but I needed to knuckle down. I wanted to be a famous film director and be the next Hitchcock. I spent the summer with the stragglers or by myself, waiting for her to come back. Writing scripts and drawing storyboards. It was great. She sent me a picture of my beads dangling on a fishing line over a crocodile. There was the Earth between us but I didn't care. I was in love and she was having fun. The two most important things in life.

Goran Ivanisevic had been picked as a wild card into Wimbledon. My adventurous girlfriend was coming home soon. I knew she wouldn't appreciate having no hot water or light when she got back after a 20-hour flight so I searched my pockets and found my last tenner. As I crossed the road to the corner shop to top up our utilities I saw that Goran's odds to win were a 1000-1. Astronomically useless odds. Unless he wins of course. Wild card? He's old now. I knew he was going to win. He'd just missed out so many times. He was hungry I could see it in him. I felt it so hard in my guts.

I screamed at the top of my voice as I handed Indian Lee my last ten pound note and he handed me back flimsy pre-pay cards that would wash and illuminate my weary girlfriend. Two weeks later she came back. Tired, smelly, she needed a bath. With the most glorious display of heart and skill, Goran won that year. If I had placed my cash on him that day I would have scooped ten thousand pounds. And of course, I'd get my tenner back.

As she soaked away thousands of miles of travel I lit her a candle, put on the radio. I smoked a joint and watched her wash her hair. When she climbed into bed with me, we kissed. Months' worth of kisses to catch up on. Her hair was sun kissed and her skin was golden brown. She told me she'd heard Goran won the tennis. I told her I didn't watch it and kissed her again. This time she described everything that was happening to her. It was the hottest thing I'd ever heard. It was quiet, it was intimate and I was the only person in the world to hear what she said.

10.

I was so angry I tried to kick their door down. Our neighbours had fallen asleep with their TV on and I had a gig the next day. I'd graduated with an award. I'd spent the last three years learning about nuance, value changes, story beats, camera techniques. My degree was in Media Production, so obviously I joined a boy band. Upstairs was a china shop. I needed to get in there and fuck everything up. How dare they keep me awake by falling asleep, it was a cruel punishment. We'd moved around together as postgrads do and she'd taken up a little part-time job. Making sure the bills were paid and debt collectors didn't come knocking. As tiny as she was I just knew things would be okay if she was involved. Her jibes and nonplussed attitude towards my mardi gras musical success kept me grounded. Her strength was unlimited. With her by my side I knew this was it. My ticket to stardom. I'd pay her back with theatre companies and vintage cars and all the cheesecake she could ever eat. In green rooms and back stages I would show roadies naughty pics I had of her on my new camera phone. Full colour. It felt good. I didn't need to stray. Totally my bird mate. Trust me. I'm a singer.

I thought I was too cool to get a proper job. Come on. I spent my days teaching kids to sing and keeping them off the streets and my nights topless in gay bars and festivals all over the country with our brand of almost amazing pop. We started out as a five piece, then the black guy left. He couldn't dance or sing. Stereotypes are bollocks. Although the muscle guy was gay as trifle. Over a course of management shuffles, dreadlocked gangsters with loaded pistols and endless showcase nights we met David, our libertine manager and producer. We settled as a two-piece electro crew. It was fun. Cernow mixed our tracks and Limahl gave us hair tips. Shows made me feel electric. Sound systems made me feel electric. Fans made me feel electric. Dancers made me feel electric. Oh, dancers. Hang on. You are electric. No, I'm not gay.

Off stage everything started to feel boring. I hadn't had to queue up for a club in years, I always got free booze and we were always just this far away from the big time. Home life became a routine. A new house. Massive town house under the airport. Two bedrooms, lots of space. Lots of space for two people doing different things. I never wanted to go out unless I was on stage. Aside from that any friends I had from before university thought I was a dick in my spray tan, Claire's Accessories bangles and vest top. Mostly ego, but it took it out of you. I was rehearsing three times a week with full PA run- throughs. Doing singing lessons twice a week and in the gym almost every day. That's what I thought you had to do. Music came first. Every promoter would ask, always at the end of our pep talk and just before we went on stage,

"You are gunna take ya top off though eh love?" Show a bit of man tits.

They didn't care about my lyrics. I was electro sausage. If you work hard it will happen. This is what I knew to be true so why wasn't it happening. The pop world was a teenage game and I was old when I started. Fuck.

When I had down time, my almost common-law wife would spend the morning shopping for delicacies and treats for me to rustle up while she soaked in the bath. I knew everything she liked. Her dreams of becoming a stage director had been put aside. The time wasn't right. We needed to pay rent and she took the nine to five. I was only just making enough money to scrape by. I'd spend my money on buying her a new TV box set or making her favourite pudding. The important stuff. She'd put a roof over my head and did the council tax. The boring stuff. It didn't matter. The big deal was just around the corner. I'd buy her everything she ever wanted and take her to see where they made Lord of the Rings. These were special days. Just us. Forty-eight hours to indulge ourselves in the privacy of our home. No work, no show, no stress, no applause. She'd shop. I'd smoke. She'd bathe. I'd cook. We'd laze. She'd dress up. I'd undress her. We'd make movies. She'd fall asleep. I'd wake up and she'd be gone.

Work meant she always got up before me. I could see it wearing her out. Hated her job. Simple. Get a new one. Easy for me to say? Of course, I'm going to be a pop star, no need to worry at all. Just around the corner. One more gig. One more demo. I can't blame her for getting bored. I'd been stuck in an almost massive phase for a couple of years now. It was best if I just didn't talk about the band. She'd heard it all before. There were things she wanted to change. Things that she needed to do. I got worried. I started to wonder. I started to wander. Her dreams can't have been that important. All that time wasted. You need to be focused if you want to make it. Love has to come second. She understood. It annoyed me that she did. Why was she so understanding? Why was it annoying me? Always working. I'd make her dinner and she'd go to bed. Her dreams were slipping away into cable TV and fantasy books. All she wanted to do was go to bed. Dancers on the other hand wanted to get drunk and naked. They had dreams. Cruise ships and Pop videos. Much better. Paying bills? Putting food in the freezer? Boring. With the flop of a closing book she'd yawn to bed. One quick peck on the lips, try not to wake her up. Something wasn't right. With the selfish mask of impending stardom, I knew that it had nothing to do with the fact that I'd watched the love of my life work herself to the bone. I played pop star to the bitter crowds of the vaporous music industry while she let her ambitions fade. Never complaining. Always supportive. Always well-presented. Always eager. Always polite. Always perfect. Totally nothing to do with me.

It took a while for her to finally tell me but I was naturally supportive. Self-esteem issues for someone so driven and beautiful with a better arse than Kylie sounded stupid to me, but if she wanted bigger boobs, then why not? We had fun with it. The thought of new clothes and massive tits made her happy. It was kinky in the consultancy room. It was the first time I'd seen another man touch my girlfriend's naked body. There was nothing sexy about the drive home. She looked like a stray cat that I'd wrapped up from the road. Every bump was pulling at stitches. The rusty little mini having no brakes, let alone suspension. They healed just fine. She loved them. Her friends from work loved them. It would be a sin not to show everyone. Night clubs are good. She'll be fine with her mates. I didn't like having to queue anyway. I'll stay at home and smoke weed by myself and wait for her to come home. Things were naughty. All those new outfits. All those new polaroids. She'd drink cocktails while she dressed up. I'd prepare a cold supper for afterwards. It was still only once a week, but the spark had returned. She was alive again.

I was making a bit of extra cash. I'd been working on the occasional film project with my Uni compadre Jan. It meant I could contribute more. I'd always been terrible with money but any day rate was better than nothing. I was on the beach in Cannes. We'd made a little film for Channel 4 and we were laughing that we were the only filmmakers to be leaving. The festival loomed, we'd be long gone. I called her from the shore. I wanted to tell her how cool Cannes was, I wanted to tell her how funny it was that we were leaving when every other film maker in the world was arriving.

"Did you know it was there?" Crackly line.

"Huh?" What you on about?

"DID YOU KNOW?" Something's not quite right.

"Hey, we're filmmakers right..." The set up.

"Why have you done this to me?!" Clearing line.

"And everyone is coming to the festival but we're..." Almost.

"For fuck sake, I found it!" Clear as day.

I had a special bag I used to take to gigs. Often we'd

stay overnight so it was worn and battered. I loved that bag. I didn't take it with me to Cannes because the strap broke. There was a little pocket created behind the zipper inside. That's where she found it.

What made it worse was that the girl across the channel was doing something nice. That's the kind of person she was. She was wearing all the low cut tops in the world and she was happy. While she was planning a little surprise for her boyfriend who was finally making a little extra money, she found a black and white picture. It was the only one I had left of the girl I'd broken. Nothing seedy, nothing kinky. Just a nice black and white photo of her, smiling. I'd dearly love to say that the reason I kept it was to remember her face before I'd turned her into stone. Before I'd alienated her from her friends as she made excuses for my erratic and violent behaviour. I'd dearly love to say that I didn't know it was there, it must have just slipped in by mistake and got lodged in a hidden pocket behind a broken zip by accident. I could feel her disappointment from across the sea. There was nowhere to run from this, besides, I was already in another country. I was coming home the next day. She'd put up with my bollocks for years and my music. Now it was time to face my own.

11.

Separate bedrooms. Keeping things polite. I'd been judging every girl that I fell in love with and comparing them to the girl in the arcade with the beaming smile. No one would ever be as beautiful. No one would ever be as perfect. It was my secret. I wanted to take the blame and ignore the details. I was comparing every girl I fell in love with to a falsehood. The girl I left behind wasn't that oxygen stealing perfect beauty from the arcade all those years ago. She was her own woman. Facing her own problems and making her own way in the world. I couldn't let it go. All I could think when I thought about her was that anyone who fell in love with her would have to know. They'd find out she would never be a mother and she'd tell them it was all my fault. That thought made me feel sick.

Sat back in our front room she told me she'd thrown the photo away. She knew who this girl with the beautiful smile was. I didn't accuse her of snooping. I believed in her motives. That was the kind of girlfriend she was. She loved doing nice things for me. I felt like such an idiot. All that time and effort and long hours and work. Humiliated. My promises were as empty as my hidden pocket behind the zipper. The weekend, worn out. All my energy into a doomed neon pink fantasy of ego and gorgeous encounters. I flopped on the settee, sparked up, cable on. Sizzle. How do they do that? Sizzle. Fizz. Light bulbs. Pop. Great I fucking love filaments. Sizzle. For fuck sake. Sizzle. What. The…

"…FUCK ARE YOU DOING!?" Spinning, shut up sizzling!

She was standing sleek in heels. Red and black Victoria's Secret corset. Perfect Danni Minogue boobs and a better arse than Kylie. She was standing in heels in front of the cooker. She was cooking me a steak. The sizzle was an expensive cut of lovely beef. I was annoyed with her for trying so hard. I was annoyed that when I turned around I missed where they kept a light bulb that had been burning for over a hundred years. I know I said something mean. Something horrible. Spoilt. I wanted to see a magic fucking light bulb you stupid steak cooking bitch! What the fuck is wrong with you? I wanted to see a FUCKING LIGHT BULB!

The black and white photo was an aesthetic nail in the coffin. I'd amazingly ignored the girl I'd spent six years of my life with who did everything in her power to make my dream come true. Going so far as to change her body with pipes and knives and operations so she felt like a woman and not a boy when I mentioned the nineteen-year-old pristine pop princesses I'd have to sing with, and pose with and dance with and kiss on the cheek. When I'd met the girl in the photo it was the best day of my young drug fuelled life.

Months of pretending. The good life. We were so jolly. I helped her find a new job. In no time she'd be running the city. In no time she'd find a knight. I had no doubt that she would be happier without me. I could see it in her eyes.

She'd always been the prettiest, funniest girl in the room. Without the make-up and the new additions, she was a lonely Princess on a boat by a leafy little bridge. She was a masterpiece and like a bitter museum cleaner, I'd just forgotten. Spotless. The house was spotless. We'd moved house so many times together we were a crack commando team. CD player on, guilt-free cheese. Little spliff. Nice bit of lunch on the kitchen table for when we finished. My lovely friends Gill and David had a loft. I had no loft. Loft it is. She'd bagged a money job. Numbers and sales. I never understood what she did. I just knew she'd be good. Final checks. Van loads and 24 hour garages. Cigarettes and singing to the radio on the motorway. Final checks. Everything gone. Final checks.

The room was bigger than I remembered. I'd been sleeping next door for months. The windows were huge. No curtains. So much light. It made my plants grow. It used to smell of perfume and body oils as much as it stank of weed. Now it smelled like an infomercial. Now there was just an unmade double bed. Now there was just me and her laying face up, side by side holding hands saying nothing. Her grip tight. Her body, ever so slightly trembling.

All those years. Even in Hong Kong on the late night streets of the fashion district she still shone brighter than everyone. Not even a retch when laughing Aunties made her eat whatever weird shit the old girls loved. After every knock-back and every 'almost' she was there. I let it fizzle away like a disillusioned cabaret act. I was always looking for better. Prettier. More amazing. More anything. Always comparing everyone to the girl in the black and white photo. The day I stole that single frame of existence it had been the single best day of my life. When the girl lying next to me on the empty bed asked me, softly, openly and honestly,

"What the fuck happened?" Silence.

I thought as days went, it was by far the worst.

12.

My loft didn't have a door. It was massive and private but mainly always open. The superhot daughter of the house was a fitness instructor. I was impressed at her dexterity and stamina. I almost fainted. Every time. I was living in an amazing house on the best road in town. The energy was positive. The life proud owners, a power house of motivation and culture. They were cool as fuck. I snuck out of the loft in taxis to massage tattooed beauties. I span bottles with excited dancers. I kissed dance school Mums at drunken parties. It was messy. I needed a break. Too many texts. Too many cock shots. Too many finger pics. Too much sauce. Way too much sauce. North. I needed to head North. I needed a break. With the money I made teaching mischievous ladies to play guitar I could afford a ticket. Trains. The only time I could ever think. When you're on a train, you're always going somewhere else. Moving. Quiet. I needed old friends.

I found refuge with old friends. They fell in love and got married after they went to university and always welcomed me with open arms, a cup of tea and a roll up. They were both beautiful, inside and out. If you lived there, you wanted to shag one of them. Possibly both, depending on which way you swung your party bat. They were honest and kind and nice and I loved them. Old fashioned pubs and cheap pints of lager made me feel like Marty McFly.

Needless sparkly bangles and the odd bit of London guy-liner made me fit right in with the locals during pie and darts night. Fuck them. I'd lived here before. I felt like the prodigal son. They'd told me that she wouldn't give a fuck that I'd hung out with Bradley from S-Club 7, she was vintage baby. If it wasn't rock and roll you were just another, "Fucking dickhead!" So cheeky.

Even through the glaze of my fifth cheap Stella I could see her Twiggy-striped eyelashes flapping. The twinkle in her eye like a Smirnoff supernova. Her hair was immaculate. She could have been on the cover of Vogue magazine in 1968 and she was nineteen years old. Shit, I'd lied about my age so much with the pop crap I'd almost forgotten. Even with the best worst guess I was nowhere near eighteen. Small town mentality. Not always a bad thing. Small towns have big faces and she was a face. A time warp of retro and so cool. So very cool. I knew she was special when we set fire to a chef's beard. I knew she was special when we spilled sauce in the back of my mate Jay's car while he drove to find us X-rated seclusion. I knew she was special when she said she knew more about music than I did.

"You know fuck all old cunt!" So much cheek.

I explained that I was actually a pioneer of electro pop. I was even a rave MC back in the 'day'. Damn it, I'd sung and played guitar on radio stations all over the world. I'd signed more worthless music management contacts than she'd had chips and mushroom gravy. How dare she. She said I wasn't Adam Ant.

"I'd fuck him so hard his stripe would come off." Pint

straight back.

Cheeky. Sexy. Same thing? Wow.

She was right. I wasn't Adam Ant. I was in the middle of my thirties, single, poor and in the world's unluckiest 'are they gay?' pop duo. I was not Adam Ant. I was no one. She made me feel like David Bowie.

I'd want to run to the train station from whatever meeting we had. A new flyer, a new demo, a new this a new that. Everything was new but just the same. I'd lived the life of a pop star. Minus the hit records, fame and the money. It all felt so fake and desperate and my retro girl was real. She was a lot younger than I was but I learnt so many things about music and fashion and history from her that I mostly felt like the youngster. I loved it. Her giggle was straight out of a carry on film. She looked like a doll. She behaved like a demon.

I considered myself adventurous. I'd travelled the world and pretended to be a movie star instead of admitting defeat. All the swagger with a worn out suitcase and a twenty pound note to my name. I'd seen things. Done things. Done things with people watching and got every 'thing' on video, after all I did have a degree in making badly lit pretentious videos. This girl scared me. I honestly wasn't sure if it was fascination or fear that made me tell her I loved her. We'd meet in cheap hotel rooms where she could let loose and laugh her head off. She'd scream that she was twelve years old. She'd been kidnapped and I was Terry Wogan. Panicking I'd try and muffle her script. It only made her more determined. Shit. I wasn't sure if what I was doing was fun or not. I really didn't want someone to boot the door down and find her dressed as a 1960s convent schoolgirl with me trying to shut her up, which by the last time we did it meant quite a firm slap on the cheek. The cheek of her, she loved it. Spice of life? It was definitely a variety I hadn't tried before. It was super chilli pepper. She'd dress me up like her favourite guitar hero from her second-hand pop magazines and do weird things to me. Taking things to the extreme is good for the soul. You can test your limits and find your place in the universe. Getting punched in the face wasn't good for the soul. Getting punched in the face wasn't even the final straw. It was the first one. Things were about to get blurry at bedtime.

It had to end. It had to end now and it had to happen today. We'd gone from award winning Ealing comedy, to slasher flick torture porn in under six months. We'd drink pints and eat pies. Her Mary Quant looked tighter. We'd drink all day, drink all night. Room service, extra hot showers. It was too intense. I was scared where it was going. It sunk so low so quickly I got bored unless she was trying to burn me with an iron while she did shots of tequila out of a shoe, but sometimes I just wanted a lovely cuddle without getting jabbed in the nose or having my bollocks electrocuted. I was a musician on his very last legs. She was a Catholic girl with danger in her eyes. I was about to tell her it was over. She was about to tell me she was pregnant. My timing as ever, was impeccable.

"Don't stop, it's okay, I'm on the pill." On. Off. One or the other.

I had time to think on the train up from Luton. I took

over from her Mum and sat in the back of the car with her as she drove us back to her house. Nice warm room, fluffy pillows. The guilt kicked in fast. At nineteen years old there was no way she wanted a baby. This didn't stop her feeling like she'd killed something. I tried to remain impartial. It was her body. There was no way I'd ever tell anyone what to do when it came to a termination. I knew that hormones make women crazy. Fuck knows what it would do to her. I edged my softly and carefully chosen words towards a life without babies. A life with a chance to at least see if babies are really the answer. We talked about how cute they'd be. We could make him a singer and he'd be like Michael Jackson and Bob Dylan. I didn't argue when she said she'd made up her mind. I told her she'd made the right choice. I grabbed my jade pendant. I thanked Buddha. I thanked Allah, I thanked every god. I stopped when I thanked Jesus. My first image of him was as a baby and it made me feel like a monster. I was slowing down. This was all too real. I was supposed to be a singer? Or was it film maker? I couldn't tell anymore. I wished the band would die. I couldn't abandon her. Not now. Fuck it.

We lasted as long as we could. Neither of us were happy. I'd come back up North to see her every few weeks. I was on the books of a nice little extras agency. Free bacon sandwiches and a good cooked dinner. I had to tell her it was over. It must have been long enough. We had a final spunk of musical progression. Maybe I'd learned something from my pop art girlfriend. I was working a lot. Film sets, TV shows, promos. I thought a lovely meal and a night at a posh hotel would be the best way to end it. Make a night of it at least. She must have known it was over. Or maybe not. After the cold and sterile three-hour trip to the clinic, her moods swung. Hot headed at her calmest she would snarl and bite at me. She must have known. There were more than one of her and I hoped they all knew. Phone calls and declarations of tablets and doses. Screaming matches until our voices were cracked and broken, my veins hurt with being pushed time and time again to the end of sanity. Pleading and pain. Guilt. Denial. Everything imploding in a single point inside her chest and I didn't care. I hadn't been this angry for so long. She reminded me of the girl with the beaming smile, the girl in the black and white photo. For fuck's sake. She was there every time. Always ready to make me feel worse. A well-deserved knife in my back for breaking the first real heart I had ever loved. The similarities hit me harder than her punch. The sleek brown hair. The screaming. The big brown eyes. The passion. The smile. The unborn baby. The cheeky smile. The unborn baby. Fuck! We were even back in the same town, only this time nearly ten years later. It took almost ten years for the news to get back to me. Nearly a decade of guilt and shame. My dark secret that I laughed off with a twisted comment in my head. How funny I am, making clever jokes about horrible things that happen to people who loved me. In the same week I broke a girl's heart, the girl who had lovingly surprised me with secret parties and silver, I heard that the girl in the black and white photo had held a party. Something to do with cycles. Something to do with time. Something to do with unbelievable. Something to do with babies. Something inside me died. Which is not always a bad thing. Was perfect, now fucked. Was fucked, now working. Relief. Was obsessed. Now free. The chains I'd visualised breaking for endless nights exploded. Fuck the chains. It had been so long since I'd seen that beaming smile. Nearly ten years had passed. I didn't need to think about her any more. I knew one day I'd let her know how sorry I was. I'd given up years ago the idea that she'd see me when I was famous on the TV and realise she missed me. Nope. I'd loved and lost. I'd loved and broken. I'd loved and learned. I'd loved and punched. Now was the time to be free. Put a flower in my hair and chill. The summer was coming. I was free. Free of a destructive relationship and free of a destructive memory. I was in an electro pop duo. We had a last hurrah, just a few more gigs. Important people in the crowd. I was about peace, vibes and bring back hippies, fuck it. I needed something pure in my life. I may even go vegetarian.

13.

I couldn't believe the level of detail in all of the costumes. It was as if I was right there, back in the Sixties. They'd even changed the markings on the road. I sat in the sun in front of the Old Bailey waiting for whatever production nightmare was happening behind scenes. I wasn't worried. It was sunny. I was going to get a free lunch and I was sat with a couple of beautiful posh blonde sisters. They looked like twins. Life was good. They laughed and swished their hair and cackled over each other's stories. The older one looked younger. Her bright green eyes twinkling at me through her greased-down flower power hair. No make-up, authentic. Scruffy hippy clothes, vintage. She didn't have a care in the world. Open and relaxed. She knew she was super hot but didn't give a public school fuck. I drank in her laid back vibe as we chatted bollocks as film extras do. Until everyone cheered. At last. Best part of the job. Lunch. It was time for lunch. On a job like this it's important to make sure you don't end up lumbered with twats. Mostly lovely people, having fun. Occasionally, twats. It's all about who you sit with when there's food on set. As I stood up and made my way towards the magic free cooked lunch I noticed something in my hand. Something familiar. Something feminine. Something with a twenty-three-year-old blonde medical student dressed as a hippy on the end of it. It was her hand. Hang on.

We were holding hands. When did this happen. Neither of us had any idea that we were holding hands. So we just kept walking. I felt giddy. Floating was easy. Groovy baby. Could have been sunstroke but either way it was trippy and hypnotic. I knew she'd noticed when her grip got stronger. She laughed as if this kind of thing happens every day. I was never letting go. I held her hand and we strolled together. I strolled right with her, hand in hand, right to the veggie section.

"It's a sign!" Summer time, when the weather is high…

"No! I always hold hands with Chinese hippies." Stretch right up…

"I'm gunna need your phone number." Touch the sky …

"And why's that?" When the weather's fine …

"Cause I'll need to call you about our wedding plans." I got women, I got women on my mind.

On our first date she'd told me that she wasn't really ready for a relationship. Messy few months. Being honest. Telling the truth. She was in bed by 8:45pm. They called the police at around 2am, I'd gone missing. They really needn't have worried. I was in bed with her. It had been a long day.

Having vodka chasers was a great idea. We were asked to leave politely. Apparently the gay bars of Soho didn't think our behaviour was appropriate. Our chemistry mixed with our ice cold chemicals had led us to 'dares'. I like a game. Kelly had taught me well all those years ago. If you wanted to win, you had to play the game properly. And that meant getting your bra out. I didn't have a bra so I showed her something else, she dared me. I dared my drunk science hippy to stoke her daring suggestion. She did. More drinks. Get your coat. More drinks. Doorway. Sunlight? Had we been there all night, getting naked in a dark and seedy corner of one of London's top fashionable haunts. We had lost ten hours of our life. Awesome. We were asked to leave again. Not so polite.

"I thought this place was edgy?" Soho. Is. Dead.

"Tolerant much?" Educated panache.

"Yeah fucking hell mate, this is a 'gay' club, let loose, be free man!" Frankie says Relax.

"This is a Wetherspoons and it's lunch time you dirty pissed fuckers now get out!" Afternoon.

We stumbled through London. She was like expensive candy floss. Her family through hard work and musical talent had connections which meant that she lived high up in a block of flats overlooking Hyde Park. One last boozer, the last bastion of Knightsbridge. One more drink. Dutch courage. We'd been kicked out of a franchised pub in the afternoon for doing things to each other and upsetting the diners. Things that you'd normally see in Amsterdam for two Euros per minute. I don't know why I thought that being in a gay club would make it okay. I guess it was the six years of working in them with my vest tops and backing tracks. Besides, she'd seemed extremely comfortable with the whole thing. What got us thrown out of this pub was the rocking motion rather than anything explicit. The Las Vegas showdown I was being treated to was knocking off all the empty glasses and bottles from the fruit machine I was leaning against. I thought the smashing sound was part of the performance. It was better than Mariah Carey, front row seats. She moved just like a Hollywood stripper with a scientific brain and she didn't dance for the money. It was glorious. It took all my strength not to giggle as the armed soldiers guarding the huge iron gate checked my ID. After a giddy lift ride twenty floors up we were in. Her parents had just gone to bed. Good job they had to get up early. It was eight-forty PM and we were both wasted. I decided that the best thing to do was get immediately naked.

Over fifty messages. Voice mails. Starting out jolly, then annoyed, then worried. Then panic. I woke up next to my gorgeous hippy science stripper. I had no idea where I was. Head thumping with yesterday's great idea. I was meant to be somewhere. Oh there's a pole in the room. Need water. Oh, there's a pole in the room. Flush. Someone's in the bathroom. When she swished in, my aches and drunken pains vanished. Masses of soft blonde wavy hair. Huge jade twinkles for eyes and not an inch of modesty.

"You're gunna have to get past the soldiers. I'm staying in bed."

"The who? Where the ..." SOLDIERS?

She shook her hair like a lioness and oozed her way back into the messy double bed. Everything about her was in the moment. The sweet scent of summer drifting all around her as she moved. It was a bit like a commercial for fabric softener it was so pure and summery. In this case it was also a little adult TV channel. As summery as she was, she was still very naked and dancing around a stripper pole. A little sauce with breakfast. Kiss goodbye. Metal lift. Clunking. Doors clang open. HORSE! Shit! Horses and SOLDIERS! The shock punched me in the brain. I had remembered that I was supposed to be in a crisis meeting with my hopeful 'gay-not-gay' pop act. This was good. They'd got worried and called the police. This was bad. After having told no one where I was going, bailed on our business plans and having turned my phone off, I had no idea why they were worried. I'd just woken up with a bonafide posh bird who lives in a London tower block guarded by soldiers. This was awesome. I waited about three seconds until I sent my text.

"See you at the show yeah?" Post tequila bravado. "Hell yeah pop star!" Sunshine and surfing posters.

I knew that it would be our last show. The hardest girl to crack had stuck by my side from the very beginning. Almost a decade ago. The fact that I hadn't even turned up for our meeting coupled with the fact that my camp neon miming partner wanted to become the next Fabio (the most beautiful man in the world) were more than smoke signals. I always loved this venue. Intimate, sexy, always rammed and loud as fuck. I wondered if the girl who made my life easy through University and beyond would be pleased that this would be the last time I donned my vest top. I swiped my eyes with the last of my mascara for extra sex appeal. It would be the last time I had to drink eight bottles of free beer just to stop me from running away. Bang in the middle of Soho. Everyone who's almost, could be, kind of someone was there. Old hats and young bucks.

Pop Show Party, London's finest showcase night and we were headlining. I couldn't wait to see my sunshine stripper. She dressed casual. Jeans wrapped tightly over her Vegas bum. Little strappy top. All eyes on her as she came to kiss me. All eyes on me when I kissed back.

"Guess he's not gay then after all?" Tittie lips.

It was a great show. They almost always were. We knew what we were doing. Photos, handshakes, shots at the bar. Velvet rope, holding hands. Running through the tube. Soldiers. Guns. Laughing. Bedroom. Bed.

"Well, you can get this lap dance here for free." NSFW.

I washed out my sonic spikes. I smeared off the faux emo make-up. I folded up my clothes and put them by the door. I took my cheap plastic bangles off. I was twenty floors up. I had the British Army downstairs with machine guns and on the night of my last ever pop show party, it was me that was getting the sexiest encore. I'd been looking for someone like this for years. By now my requirements for a perfect match were so intricate they were almost impossible to reach. Almost. I had stopped being addicted to looks alone years ago. Each and every girl I had fallen in love with, to me had been the most beautiful. Why else would I have been attracted to any one less than that? They didn't need to be beautiful, they needed to have magic powers.

"Ah, who cares, early late. Same thing huh?" Kiss. Blow.

Her aura was so breezy I felt like a three-year-old with a new pot of bubbles. This girl was perfect. This girl was stunning. This girl was clever. This girl had an ex-boyfriend.

"Just so you know, I still have fee …" Honesty. Kiss.

"Too bad for him! What a loser!" Kiss. Shit.

Nothing was going to get in my way. So what if they'd been together for years? So what if he cheated on her? So what if she still had feelings for him? I was prepared to do and say anything to make sure that she fell in love with me. It was almost a week since I'd met her. This was taking ages. Sat in my loft I curled around my phone like a teenage girl. The only picture I had of her was from a cheeky photo shoot for a new bar in Mayfair. It was hot. I had to show everyone.

I never really understood dating. Having grown up watching Hollywood teens angst their way through puberty I just saw it as a huge waste of time. Why wait? Why ever wait for anything if it's right there in front of you. Our first date ended up like a Prodigy video. Our second date took us to Brighton. Screw you Smallville. We'd both been asked to come in for a photoshoot for a little talent agency, extra work, walks-ons. We spent the morning in front of flash bulbs, the afternoon looking at the diamonds of the dead in old Harry Potter windows and the evening on the warm stony beach.

"Nah, they won't care, they live in Brighton." The whole world setting behind her.

"I'm sure they can see my c …" Coat for modesty.

It was rude. We were behaving like the locals. The waves crashing. The sky purple and yellow behind her easy beauty as she undressed me. The small crowd of people who could obviously see everything. It was amazing. I felt like the star of a French movie. One where everything just works and nothing much happens. A small part of me would have appreciated a cheer. Two days later she told me.

"I can't see you for a while." Carefree?

"Oh, that's cool ..." NO! NO! NO!

"I just need to breathe." Past life creeping.

We all have history. I've never had patience. My stripping beauty had dropped the ex-bomb. Disaster. My normal course of action would be extreme B movie anger. How dare she refuse the chance of real love? I'd known her for a week for God's sake! Come. On. Perhaps it was the vision of her I had burned into my retina. A vision of her sat atop me. Our exhibition. The sky, a tantric mess of everything cheesy. Her heart-stopping smile. Possibly a mixture of everything. Something strange happened. Something unusual. For the first time in my life I listened to what she was saying and I knew she was telling the truth. Until now I knew that everything a girlfriend said would at some stage become a ballache. Flirty conversations that were joined with bird song became hideous displays of extreme stupidity.

"Yes!" NO

"NO!" yes!

"Go." STAY

"I love you." I HATE YOU.

I would concoct the most vicious insults. I hated everything they loved. I despised the very thing that I fell in love with. It was nasty. I was shameless. I could never accept that some things just don't work. Stupid. I'd seen every significant relationship fail. My Parents and my Grandparents. My girlfriends always had a story. My best friends kept dying. I kept wanting better. Why was I always so surprised each time?

"…You know what?" Sunset.

"…Do what you have to do …" Calm.

"…You've got my number …" Wife.

In a whole life of romantic fantasy, I'd never done the right thing before. I'd done the rashest, most unreasonable thing. I saw a light bulb. That fucking lightbulb. It was right here all along. She said she'd call me in a few weeks. I would have waited years for her to send the text. I waited one hundred and forty-four hours. Maybe this time. The right way. The right time. The right choices.

Life in the poshest tower block in the world was indulgent. They were all veggies. Adventurous veggies, always something new and delicious. They swapped meat for crunch and chilli and cream and spices. Healthy comfort food. Double win. My dreams of popular stardom were over. Kaput. I'd thrusted my hips a million times on stage and still didn't have a pink Lamborghini. Fuck it. I couldn't give a shit. I'd been on a low fat diet for years. I could teach box aerobics pissed and blindfolded I'd done it so many times. I let my hair grow. I bust my shoulder and quit the gym. We drank milkshakes with vanilla ice cream from Harrods. We chomped on expensive Shazaan curries and homemade breads for sandwiches. I'd wait for my sunshine blonde to come home and throw fifty pound notes at me after a sordid shift. We'd sneak up to the top deck and stare at the lights of the whole of London while I smoked a sneaky spliff with two hundred soldiers asleep below me. Life was good. We walked everywhere. We talked everywhere. We kissed everywhere. We held hands everywhere. I got a bit fat.

She was doing a Masters in nutritional science. I loved that she was cleverer than me. I only had a Bachelors. I loved that you would never in a billion years guess she wasn't just a teenager's wet dream come true. She was Charlie's Angel. Money wasn't tight. Her part-time evening job sorted that out. It made me feel like a rock star knowing she was stealing money from footballers and bank managers and spending it with me. I trusted her. When she told me something I believed her. She made me feel that I could tell her anything. We walked, we talked, we laughed, we high-fived after everything nice that happened.

When she said she couldn't come I didn't understand. We were going on a huge adventure. One thousand miles across China. She loved travelling, she loved new things. Shit, she was my sunshine stripper scientist.

"Why not?" Silly Billy.

"Because, because of my ex." Always honest.

I'd been living in a post-pop haze for a while. We'd spent summers overseas and winters on the slopes with everything in the middle. I'd been making a little cash, calling on the good will of my production friends. I'd taken little steps back into the world of cameras and editing for money. The clarity of what she said was hard to take. Even after all this time. She feared that she would break free of our loving party and seek him out. He was in China studying.

"It's a pretty big country." I'm sure you won't bump into him.

Material things didn't impress her. One valentine's day I had an idea. I strung a curtain across the room and hung a bed sheet over it dividing the room in two. I had a big box of crafting bits and bobs. Coloured paper, glitter, glue and pens. I set my alarm for half-an-hour and we made each other gifts from the fluff and sparkles. It was beautiful. When the curtain came down and we presented each other with our creations, we felt like we'd smacked Clinton cards right in the minge. Not that she'd ever smack anyone, she was tranquil and calm, but as serene as she was, she was deadly. Hidden behind her Shakira wolf, she was as cunning as a fox. She knew exactly what power she held over men. She would melt when I kissed her and whoop. The whoop of a rich girl who's just hit a hole in one from a yacht. So independent, so sure. It was intoxicating. I'd watch her as she sat, wrapped in a towel. Tired of endless hours of reading science journals. She'd take my hand and we'd dance on the bed. I'd get a free lap dance with all the extras. I'd make her a low fat macro biologically beneficial snack and she'd read till sunrise. I adored her. Why was she so sure she'd run back into his arms?

"I can't trust myself not to try and find him." Real tears.

She hardly ever cried. I'd learned to breathe. I'd learned to wait until the sentence was over before I tattooed my declaration of hate on my face. I had no idea what this meant. We needed to have a break. Oh yeah, I was going to China, without her. While she stayed and cried over her cheating ex. Great. I'd let her go before. The adage of setting the ones you love free kicking me in the nuts. I'd done it once before. I'd done the right thing. I had no choice this time. It would be weeks before I saw her again. I told her I was in love with her within a month, which felt like an eternity. I'd let her have her space. She said she needed time to think. She was a clever girl. I hoped it wouldn't take too long.

While I was away, the ex had come back to London. They'd talked. I never understood the fascination with him but then the new boyfriend never does. He'd cheated on her with a girl she knew. Unfinished business. I'd hoped that the time apart and the freedom to explore the fall-out would make everything alright again. Luckily, it did.

When it got too hot in the city we'd take off our shoes and socks and splash around the Diana memorial in Hyde Park. The cold soothing water mixed with the piss of a hundred toddlers. It was bliss. We'd talk about everything. Her science facts used to fascinate me. She was the perfect blend of brain and tart. She is without doubt the 'one'. At first her honesty was hard to deal with. Normally when you ask a girlfriend if there's anything wrong,

"You okay hunny? Anything I can get you?" General concern.

"I'm fine." Three hours later you'll get it in the neck.

With her it was more, "You okay hunny? Anything I can get you?" General concern.

"No, I was a bit annoyed when you were doing (insert bad thing)." Straight out.

"Oh, sorry, are you mad at me?" Offer neck.

"No. Just saying." Kiss.

Strange, so strange. In almost all of my other relationships I suffered the reading of minds phenomena. Why didn't I know exactly what the problem was by being sensitive? Why the fuck did I not realise that you were actually really hungry, after offering to cook dinner or get a takeaway? Obviously the problem was with me. Me, boys, men, males in general. Having a straight answer was frightening. Having a straight answer meant that there was nowhere to hide. You can't hide behind a shouting match in the middle of the street when your questions are met with the truth. I couldn't believe my luck. Finally, I had found a woman who could communicate with no caveats. No hidden agenda, nothing being tested. The freedom it gave the relationship was amazing. As honest as she was, I was too. There were some uncomfortable moments, especially when having to go through the finer points of her month long 'ex-capade', but once things are out in the open you have a choice. You can choose without malice or expectation, how to engage.

The last time we were in Brighton together, we had sauce on the beach. That most magnificent erotic display on the pebbles of the English Riviera. This time we were moving house. Having vicariously lived the life of an Arabian Prince for the past couple of years made me turn my nose up at the new place. Students. Students everywhere. I ended up loving it purely based on the fact that it's always nice seeing someone getting a pint of milk in a zebra onesie at three AM, but the house was in need of a spruce. I'd stated quite clearly (using my new skills of straight talking), that this place was a "Shit hole". Paint?

Her bright green eyes convincing me that it wasn't. I put up her new curtains and helped her erect her stripper pole. She'd quit the late night low brow cash cow to finish her Masters. I respected her for that. It always amused me how clever she was. Only because I saw her so often in her seven inch heels, her sliver sparkly dress, her hair Baywatch blonde and eyes smokey. I used to feel sorry for her punters.

"Wanna buy me a drink?" I'll be emptying your bank account in two shots of cheap bubbles mate.

Books and books and papers and websites and notes and CDs and videos of lectures. We'd walk through the lanes and look for antique treasures. Late night sessions at the twenty-four-hour DVD machine. Breakfast, lunch, dinner, supper. Vegetarian admittedly, but as delicious as she was. By now I was sure she was the one. Her parents were sweet, musical and scientific. Caring to a tee. We talked about our wedding. How amazing it would be. Screw the norm. Let's have a Narnia theme event where guests have to search through a magic cupboard and find our union of love surrounded by lions and witches. I'd have to ask her Dad first of course. He was a military man, musical, but still military. He was a generous and gentle man. This would be easy.

"I would like permission to ask for your daughter's hand in marriage." Sir.

The new paint was on. The damp was under control. Tuesday night. I couldn't sleep. Something was wrong. Something felt wrong inside my body. Not matters of the heart but physical things. She took me to a drop-in centre where an Indian doctor inspected places with a rough un-gloved finger.

"Take a pain killer, you'll be fine." Next patient please!

I wasn't fine. Twenty-four-hours later, I was very not fine.

"But you said I needed an operation?" WTF.

"I'm the registrar and I say you can go home." Billy big bollocks.

I'd been prepped for an operation. I was on the bed ready to go. My science girlfriend knew what they were saying deciphering their clipboard code. Sticking up for me she explained the situation. I'd lost half a stone in weight in a week, hadn't slept for just as long. When I got back to her house she made me a delicious snack. Anything that she could do to make my life better she did it. She kept me warm, and she cooled me down. She cooked me food that would boost my immune system, she stayed by my side. Reading her homework and making sure I was okay. Later that night I had managed to teeter to the loo. Sweating, sick feeling, dizzy, blood. Lots of blood. Panic. Ambulance. Fuck you, registrar.

I woke up wearing stockings and a nappy. Odd. I couldn't remember anything. A nurse brought me a cup of tea and a diazepam and told me to relax. Five seconds later the curtain was swished back. A small group of students were doing rounds.

"Do you mind if we just take a peek?" Professional.

"Peek away Doogie Howser." Drugs and tea leaves.

Swish. Curtain. Swish. Sunshine. She had come to make sure I was okay. I'd had to have an emergency procedure to remove an infected blood clot I'd earned after a radical slam on a snowboard. I slammed on my bottom. The blood clot had amusingly chosen the worst place to get infected. Scooping out flesh in case of the bad blood spreading to good tissue left me clogged up with dressings. Everyday dressings. Six weeks. Everyday. I only found out it was going to be so long after my first appointment.

"Cool. So that was a little bit fucking embarrassing. Am I done now?" Pulling up my pants very, very slowly.

"No, you need to book for tomorrow." Not phased.

"Cool, so couple days, be right as rain yeah?" Almost up.

"Couple of days? You need to have your dressings changed for six weeks." No memo.

"Cool, that's fi … WHAT!?" The hell!

My Brighton bliss was blighted. Six fucking weeks. I couldn't even walk let alone work. Every day she woke me up. Made me breakfast. Nutritionally balanced, tasty and effective. She'd sit while I showered in case I fell over. Every day she would help me into a taxi and shuffle me to the room of doom. I had taken my trousers down so many times I forgot that some of the nurses didn't know what was wrong with me.

"Morning." Pants down.

"And you are?" Check the notes.

"Ah." Pants up quick.

Having the science background came in handy. She ordered me supplements, researched how to help me heal. When I got frustrated with my arse-ache of a problem she calmed me down. She danced on her pole and I watched while I swallowed pain killers, antibiotics and grilled artichoke salad.

Her studies were coming to an end. Let's celebrate. Let's go away. Her Mum offered to pay for us to go on holiday. A big deal. Her sisters and their respective boyfriends were coming along as well. A proper extended family unit. Please let me heal by then. As the holiday crept ever closer I knew that there was no way I'd be totally healed. I was worried that I'd be a slow lumbering burden but I wanted a holiday with my girlfriend.

"Naaaaah! I'm like totally like okay with it yah." Science brain.

The nurse explained how to change the dressings. Explaining the do's, don'ts sand fuck no's. A little green bag with surgical packets. Red crosses and green squares, pills, pills and more pills. Life had got weird. Laying in an immaculate Spanish villa while your girlfriend puts things in your private places would normally have been fun. Not this time. It was painful and uncomfortable. I could see in her face and hear the tiny cracks in her voice. How much more could she put up with? The answer was all of it. She never complained once. Always looking on the bright side. Not a posh care in the world.

A few weeks after we got back, I had finally healed. Given the all clear by the doctors I went back to my loft. I'd been in her room for over six weeks. It felt strange being by myself. I couldn't believe how much effort and energy she'd given me. Especially at such a crucial time in her education. This girl was simply an angel and now more than ever I knew that I wanted to marry her. We'd talked about it a lot. I'd teach the kids how to sing and skateboard, she'd teach them about diets and healthy eating. Posh and Becks can suck our boobs. Having spent almost six years studying she deserved a proper break. Our holiday in Spain had been nice, but I know it would have been better without the DIY surgery and grumpy patient.

"Wanna go to Vietnam?" Six weeks free of charge.

"Well ..." Don't they eat dogs?

Her and a group of student stripper buddies were going to have a final hurrah before they knuckled down and got scientific. I'd never really been that bothered about travelling for the sake of it. I'd been lucky enough to see the world through family and work so the prospect of back packing didn't seem that fun at first. 'Stripper buddies' was a phrase that rattled around my brain for a while. Me, my amazing clever gorgeous girlfriend and four of her late night man swindlers? The prospect of back-packing suddenly became exciting. I was completely healed. I could leap and run and climb. Of course I want to go.

"Boom! Count me in!" Summer rolls. I'll try a bit of puppy when the veggies aren't looking.

I had never really wanted to see anywhere other than Hong Kong when I travelled East. I never saw the point of trailing around an Oriental third world country, but a free trip with a gang of clever hotties was too good to turn down. I even got a phrase book. I'd been living back at my loft for a few weeks. It was weird not being with her every day. My routine of wake up, shower, taxi, pants off, pain, pants up, taxi, lunch, bed was thankfully long over. The sun was shining again.

I didn't have to bare my bits to friendly-faced, over-worked nurses anymore and I was looking forward to my backpacking adventure. I hopped on the train to Brighton. I couldn't wait to see her and show her my new awesome Vietnamese phrasebook.

"We need to talk …" Serious voice.

"Cool, I'll be there soon …" The sun has got his hat on.

"No, I don't think you should come …" Something final.

"But, I'm on my way …" Three stops to Brighton. Please not now.

I knew from the tone of her voice that something had changed. All I wanted to do was see her, be excited with her about our trip. I'd had a turnaround, I'd cheered up. I was looking forward to it. I wasn't even going to complain that it wasn't Hong Kong and I certainly wasn't worried about her ex anymore. I'd spent the last two months by her side and I was confident that she was over him. She hadn't mentioned him for a long time. What was happening? We were perfect together. That smile, those eyes, her soft curly hair, her carefree posh not giving a fuck and her sexy secret stripper night life. My guts turned into a cauldron of shit and piss. Rusty nails and puke. What was happening? I didn't understand it. It made zero sense to me. I was going to ask her to marry me and I was certain that she'd say yes. Her Dad was a Household Cavalier for fuck's sake, we could have got married at St Paul's Cathedral.

"I'm so sorry." Real tears.

"WHY!" Shoot me now.

"I just don't think we'll end up together." Scientific.

This was a blow to my nuts. I begged and pleaded. We'd overcome the ex-factor. I'd set her free and she flew back. She'd let me see that I could be honest in a relationship. She'd taught me that talking was good and that listening was even better. I'd trusted her in her heels and I'd learned that punching a letch in a night club was wrong, even if he had groped her arse on the dance floor in front of me. I'd grown as a man and I'd grown as a human. What the fuck was wrong? Three years of holding hands. Three years of knowing what each other was feeling. Three years of kissing and walking and talking and being in love. Over. All over. A week before we were all meant to be leaving on a jet plane to the muddy streets of Vietnam.

"I have to end it I'm so sorry." Conclusion.

"No please, please no." Something was dying.

"I need to be on my own." Trigger. Pulled.

She explained to me that she did love me. She explained to me that she'd thought about her future and that I wasn't in it. We hardly ever argued. We hardly ever fought. Maybe that was the problem. Or maybe the problem was that in her educated mind I just didn't fit in. Her ex-boyfriend was Chinese. Had I just been a replacement? Had I just been a twisted reminder of the cheating man who broke her heart? When she told me that she wasn't ready for a new boyfriend when I met her, I didn't care. I was full of ego and as cocksure as a millionaire playboy. All I knew was that on one sunny day sat in front of the Old Bailey we'd held hands dressed as hippies, and that was enough for me to know that she was perfect.

"You can still come with us." She'd bought the ticket after all.

There was no way I could go with them. It felt as if someone had died. Gill, who owned the loft, told me that having your heart broken was like grieving. She was right. I blubbered into my pillow so no one could hear me. When I woke up I couldn't breathe. I stopped eating. I stopped doing anything. I drank coconut rum until I wanted to puke sweet bile or fall asleep. The only good thing was it tasted the same on the way out as it did the way in. All I could think about was her in another country surrounded by hunky young buck 'Trustafarians'. Each one just as carefree as she was. Just as single. It drove me mad. I spent months in my loft in tears. Weeks and weeks in my loft drinking anything I could swipe, anything I could put down my throat to stop me from thinking.

"Time." Gentle.

"Time." Will happen.

"Time." Healing.

Time heals all wounds. Bullshit cliché. Unless you have your leg cut off. True. The thing about time is that it passes no matter how hard you try to slow it down or speed it up. I was ashamed. I was ashamed I wasn't good enough for her. I was ashamed that I knew that my temper had gotten the better of me and made her doubt me. She'd let me off because I was ill. I was recovering. I was ashamed that she only let it go on until I had healed and moved back to my rooftop cave. I was ashamed that I was so sure that she'd say yes when I asked her to marry me. I was ashamed that I was in my mid-thirties, single and crying in a loft with no

door. Gill, the lovely lady of the house asked me if I'd ever
done gardening before.

"Well, yeah, quite a lot actually, um why?" I'm just
sneezy, hay fever.

"Wanna dig up the patio?" All the jollies, and all the
answers.

The garden of the house was stunning. Topiary, bee
keeping and fresh fruit. The days when I was in love with
my sunshine stripper but apart from her, I'd laze in the sun
and Gill and I would chat about hockey and pop music.
Gill was the coolest granny on the block. I'd often find her
in the kitchen rocking out to Led Zeppelin, her husband
Dave was a proper geezer. They met at art school. A
Del Boy, but he wasn't waiting for next year. He was off
making his next big buck and riding a scooter without a
care in the world right now. They were inspirational, kind,
generous and always right.

"You want me to dig up the patio?" Just to clarify.

"Grab a pickaxe and a sledge hammer and smash the
hell out of it!" Green fingers. Wise.

"Really? But why?" Unsure, but the tunnel was lit.

"We fancy a change, bored of the crazy paving." Nod
to the tool shed.

I spent the next few days splitting rock with iron in the
blazing sun. Each and every strike deafening my stupid
misery for a split second. It was good. My hands were
blistered and my back was burning. I didn't give a shit. It
was something to concentrate on and it got me out of my
stinky bedroom. A madman taking out his broken heart
on broken slabs of ugly grey concrete. I worked hard

and I worked fast. Shit. What now? I can't smash up the driveway, how will Dave get his mod scooter up?

"Put your music on and go for a run" A bee keeper's sage advice.

Fuck it. What did I have to lose? I'd let myself go. The boyband diet of ego and vest tops had turned into a diet of cake and crying. My hair was long and unkempt. No more ultra-strong moulding clay. I was a chunky muppet who'd let the woman of his dreams run as far away as she possibly could. I didn't need this. I pulled out some old jogging bottoms. I tied my trainers on tight and I ran. I ran in circles. I never knew Luton had such amazing parks. Running in circles with my music blaring. Rave music. No pop. No cheese. Hardcore rave. I downloaded a mix from the world's best DJ and pressed play.

'Casual Breakin'. Music to change your mood.

I ran every day. I listened to the same rave mix. The beats and the bass line thumping along in time to my heavy footsteps. The music brought back my fight. The music filled me with power. As I jogged around the park in ever increasing circles I started to feel better. With each huff and puff I was healing and I didn't have to pull my pants down once. Things were looking up finally.

"You're going to need to move out. We're selling the house." Young boys need their Grandma.

I was used to moving. I'd moved almost as many times as I'd blown out birthday candles. Shit. Where do I go? I'd lived off their generosity for much longer than I should have. They looked after me when I had sunk to my lowest. They were downsizing and a half-Chinese lodger living in the roof wasn't going to go down that well with the new owners.

"Come and stay with me for a bit." I'm your little Brother. "We got a massive house." All grown up. "It'll be great!" All those Jackie Chan films. "I'll come and get you." I wanted to cry.

While I had spent my life falling in love, my little brother had become a man. He was living in Leeds and teaching Martial Arts. A huge house in the middle of a bustling student area. He promised parties and multiplayer gaming. Halloween dress up and late night rock band sessions. Kung Fu training and intense action. He told me,

"I've started cheerleading!" For the skills of course.

I laughed. I laughed from my belly for the first time in what felt like millions of years. I pictured him in purple and silver lycra holding pom-poms instead of nun-chucks. It made me laugh out loud. He'd assured me that the reason that he'd taken up the sport was the back flips, the tumbling and the acrobatic skills. I'd always packed light. I'd moved so many times I knew that I only needed a few things. I didn't own any furniture; I didn't own a fridge. I threw away all my tight boy band clothes and deleted any trace of my failed pop career. The North was calling. He picked me up and I waved goodbye to my doorless triangular space. He'd made me a little room in the garage and we stayed up late playing video games and eating chicken and broccoli. Chicken and broccoli is good for the soul and my soul needed feeding. He told me that he had a cheerleading meeting on the Sunday and that I should come along and film his first competition.

As I stood in a sports hall laughing at my little Kung Fu brother dressed in silver and purple lycra, I didn't see any pom-poms. Instead I saw two-hundred university girls in hot pants and figure hugging spandex flipping and flying through the air. I thought about my summer sunshine stripper scientist. I thought about her for just under one second. Cheerleaders. I thought about them for a lot longer than that. I wasn't ready to fall in love. Not after I'd been so devastated. Not after I'd spent so many weeks in tears smelling of Malibu and crème de menthe, running around in circles listening to rave tapes. No way. I was here to have fun. I was here to spend time with my brother and get back on track. Get my arse back in shape and Kung the fuck out of the Fu. Cheerleaders. They looked so sexy in their spankies. Cheerleaders. Smiling after every tumble and pose. Cheerleaders. Co-ordinated displays of positivity and fun. So what if it was a bit 'good ol' US of A'? So what if it was ever so slightly pervy? I for one thought that being cheery was exactly what I needed to do. I was too old and fat to join in, I knew that. I also knew that I was also slightly pervy.

"We're all going to the Uni bar, wanna come?" Gimme a drink. DRINK!

Surrounded by a hundred girls pumped up from being thrown twenty feet in the air and having techno mixes blasted out non-stop for hours. Pints of beer for a pound. I was as far away from my old life as I'd ever been. My music dreams were well and truly laid to rest. My heart was a bag of loose Lego and cat shit. I wanted to start again. I'll start at the bar.

14.

My little Brother had taken up cheerleading to add pizzazz to his bag of tricks. I understood this. Having seen how crazy and aggressive it actually was, I saw the value. While I was there I saw more people getting bloody in lycra than in black belts. It worked the same the other way. A couple of the university team thought that taking up Kung Fu would give them an extra bit of pop. Training was great. It made me forget. It took all the shame and guilt I felt for each and every one of my failed attempts at the 'good life' away for a couple of hours, plus my belly was taking the piss.

My younger sibling has always had a flair for the celebratory things in life. Halloween is a tacky American sweet selling juggernaut but a great excuse for a party. We'd hired in black lights and sprayed horrible things on the walls. We had a spooky room set up with horror films projected on a creepy loop and tombstones in the garden with our names on. He was excited about lasers. So was I. We had lasers. He'd even taped dead body chalk outlines on the floor for added creepiness. She was laying on the floor like a dead body when I first saw her.

"Look alive darling." I'm funny.

"Zed's dead." Not square.

Bright wig. Black one-piece bodysuit. Frothy blood coming out of her nose. All the detail. A tiny Tarantino dream girl. She was in my brother's cheer team. She was there with her best friend from back home. It's hard to tell what someone looks like when you've had three bottles of fizzy wine and you're wearing sunglasses in the dark but I really, really liked the detail. A lot.

"She's got a boyfriend." She's got a busy-body mate.

Hands off. Instant. Ah well. Never mind. I was here to get my head straight. I'm not here to fall in love. Fuck that. I'm not even here to have random sex with students, but when I heard her laugh, it was like none of the pain and suffering had ever existed. It was the giggle. Her tiny little infectious giggle. Standing no more than five feet high. Jumble sale couture artisan fashion. Underneath the costume she was a mini Marilyn Monroe. Design student, second year. She was a flyer. She'd started Kung Fu because she thought it was cool and she wanted to learn how to kick ass. Her soft Barnsley accent and little shrug was magnetic. I knew that I was in no fit state to pimp out my soul again but I was living the student life. Get out there and do things. So I did.

Standing in my brand new Kung Fu T-shirt, medium, still tight on my guts, I heard that musical laugh. Lovely. The Halloween girl was in the sports hall. She was wearing the same T-shirt as me. Classmates. I loved how she kicked and punched with such aggression. Each punch and kick was accompanied with the cutest little squeak. She was adorable. She was also hard to get by herself. Her best friend from home keeping a beady eye on my untrustworthy charm. Work hard, play hard. That's what people say. I'd spent two hours trying to breathe through a series of legs and arms and chops. I'm half-Chinese so when it comes to any kind of martial art I have to represent. Even if it means I almost faint and puke.

"Looks like you need a cuppa tea." Milk one sugar.

"I'm fine, I'm just too old." Oxygen is good.

"You're never too old for a nice cuppa tea." Those giggles.

Her giggle made me feel like I was thirteen-years-old again. It was a shame was that even though I felt like a thirteen-year-old, I looked like a wheezing out of shape man in his mid-thirties playing student and living in my little brother's garage.

"Outhouse, tonight. We can all play Rock Band?" We had all the plastic bits and bobs.

"Sure, why ever not?" Hollywood giggle.

"Won't your boyfriend mind?" I was always a fan of screen sirens.

"No, he's a doosh." Press start to play.

It was fun. Fun in its purest sense. No drugs, no egos, no dance floors. Just a house full of Kung Fu guys and cheerleaders all mashing the hell out of plastic instruments with no neighbours to worry about and having the best time ever. I hadn't been this happy for months. I'd try and engineer an empty seat so she'd have to sit next to me. Her ever beady-eyed best friend from home making sure that I wasn't corrupting her. I admired what she was doing. They were all from the same town. They'd known each other for years. She was just looking out for her friends. She was the law maker and I was the new kid in town and I was in no way shape or form going to get the girl with the giggle alone by myself. Must be a Uni thing.

Christmas was fast approaching. I always get particularly romantic at this time of year. By now my Mum and Stepdad had endured countless 'surprise guests' on the big day. I'd lay on thick the allure of a country style Christmas. Logs on every open fire. Hot chocolate. Snuggles and kisses under the tree. No wifi, no phone signal, just us, wrapped up warm eating cheese and crackers and drinking gin cocktails with our lovely old cat Bonnie, who can flop at will. Who could resist?

The town was lively. German markets and tankards full of beer. Our Kung Fu team was sharing the merriment with our cheerleading counterparts. A man played electric guitar on a table and fireworks shot out from his fret board.

"Nightcap?" Twinkly lights.

We all came back to the house together. High on festive cheer. Plastic guitars in hand. Wine in boxes. It being the season to be jolly we played charades. Keeping the next clue secret, we went in pairs into the kitchen to whisper our film, play, books. Two words, first syllable, sounds like cat.

At last. A chance to get her on her own. The rules of the game meant that her best friend from home had to stay in her seat. Her judging eyes held back by parlour game rules. We toppled into the kitchen. She giggled, that music box giggle. I leaned in to whisper in her ear. I could feel the warmth of her body as I got closer. In my mind I was going to say,

"Oranges are not the only fruit." Movie brain.

But instead she looked up at me and we touched Christmas lips.

"Ooh, that was lovely." Fizzy.

With bellies full of cheap red wine and real mince pies we stole kisses out of sight of her best friend from home. The rules said that we had to leave the room, to give each other the next clue. The rules said that we had to be quiet, so no one would get a head start. The rules said that we had to lean into each other so close that only we could hear each other's gentle whisper. The rules said that we had to snog each other's faces off when we should have been thinking about clever film titles that weren't just film, one word, one syllable, sounds like …

"Jaws!" Points to face.

It was perfect. In fact, if we hadn't come back into the room with a cheeky grin and a secret, we'd have been playing the game badly. Her best friend from home wouldn't know a thing. Ha and fuck you, I got a degree already. The thing about students is that occasionally they have to study. When I did my degree I watched films, played with video tapes and flight cases full of broken old shit. The pressure wasn't high. Her best friend from home was studying law. Serious. She wanted to be a judge.

"Come on you, I got lectures all day tomorrow." You may now stand up and leave the house.

"I think she's fallen asleep?" Cunning.

"Oi, you lazy cow! I don't want to walk home on my own." Friends can slap friends in the head.

No movement. Shake. Second Slap. Shout. Nothing. Just the tiny rise and fall of her art house Christmas jumper. Interesting. We hadn't planned a secret sleep over. We hadn't agreed to hoodwink her most lawful and investigative best friend from home. Shit, maybe she had just fallen asleep. If she had, would I actually have more fun with her friend? I'd always fancied the girls in Ally McBeal, they were high-flying legal types. They had an air about them. Sexy.

"You know what? Let her sleep here, I'll walk you home." Point at the settee. Hiccup.

"Oh, okay, yeah she'll be fine." Courtroom confidence.

"Yeah fuck her, she's only doing art, you're gunna be a lawyer!" Ego your honour.

"Ha, yeah fuck her. Let's go." Best friends forever.

I walked her through the cold streets of Leeds. There had been an ice storm, the worst one for decades and it had frozen the North of England to the core. I'd never been so cold in my life. The journey should have taken ten minutes but we had to Bambi step our way. I had no idea where we were going, deeper into the student suburbs. Each late night corner shop that offered cheap cider and electricity cards morphing into the next. The snow and ice made everything quiet. It was magical. Cold but magical. The legal beagle to be was beautiful, brown eyes and blonde hair, body fit from trampolining her way to medals in her youth. Blonde hair and brown eyes. The unusual combination, but like her sleeping art student buddy she was taken. They both had boyfriends from back home too. They'd been together forever. I tested the water.

"University is about letting go of your old life, evolving, moving forward." Plan. Formulating.

"Nah. I'll marry him." Sensible girl.

I believed her. Why not? I still challenged her notions of

love and romance. She had answers. Good ones. I thought that she'd make an excellent lawyer so I skirted around the subject of going back home and trying to shag her sleepy buddy. I mean, this was the plan right? Or was it? I'd been told on more than one occasion that evening that she 'had a boyfriend' so there was no chance surely?

"He's a bit of a dick to her sometimes. He'd rather hang out with his mates." New evidence for the case.

Ha. My moral inroad to infidelity. If he was a dick to her, then surely he wouldn't mind if I shared a little squeeze of sauce with his girlfriend from back home. Plus, now he could go and hang out with his new exciting university mates without worrying about her. He could use the time to grow his hair, or join a band and get famous. Either way, his girlfriend was asleep on my brother's sofa. Her best friend from home was stood in front of her own front door and her boyfriend was being a dick with his pals. I was basically doing everyone a favour.

I would have run back to my snoozy art student as fast as I could but it was too slippery. My face frozen in a silly grin. I had no idea how long I was going to be living here but I knew that moments are to be seized, not ignored. I'd spent my whole life falling in love and being heartbroken. I was here to have fun. I was here to have fun with art lovers and cheerleaders. Being single didn't matter anymore. I was a student again. Admittedly a 'mature' student that wasn't registered or even attending classes, but I had all the time in the world and zero fucks of which to care about. Finally escaping the breath- stealing cold I snuck into the living room. I snuck quite loudly.

"Oh, hello Mister." Curling awake like a cat.

"Wanna sleep in a cosy bed tonight with me?" Red light bulb, heater on since the afternoon.

"But I'm already cosy right here." Resistance at ten percent.

"Your boyfriend won't want you sleeping on a couch?" Think of your posture.

"He won't care. He's probably shagging his boyfriends." This is it.

"Cup of tea when you wake up?" Leaning in.

"Milk and no sugar." I'm sweet enough.

"I wonder if I can pick you up?" Back don't fail me now.

"Well. I am only tiny." That giggle. Oh that giggle.

We spent the next few weeks pinching kisses away from prying eyes. Eyes that were lawful and correct. Eyes that wouldn't be too impressed with our educational infidelity. It made it much more exciting. I didn't feel that bad until I met the guy. He was a nice lad. Twelve years younger than me and his whole life ahead of him. He was your typical 'cool' kid. He had the hair and the skinny jeans. I had grey bits and his girlfriend's knickers in my room. As contentious as it is, there's something extra naughty about cheating with someone. Each touch, each look, each glancing stroke is amplified. It puts life through a sexy adventure filter and besides they weren't married. No kids were going to lose a parent or grow up punching dogs in the guts because of Mummy and Daddy not loving each other anymore.

"He won't find out." Or will he?

Intrinsically it's a bad thing. It's mean and selfish. It will always cause trouble. I can't think of many long term relationships that people have had that started with cheating. Now there's nothing to say that's impossible but any chance of real love should start from a base of purity and honesty. What makes the whole thing so exciting is the chance you might get caught. Time is fleeting. Devour the minutes. Eyes are watching. Secret signals. Pressure mounting. Explode in silence. I'd smoked a cigar with her boyfriend once. Parties. Every night. I quite liked him. Normal, young man being a young man but his girlfriend was bored, she wanted something else. Maybe I should have told him, I normally like to help where I can. We had an angle. We'd train hard in Kung Fu, hit the bar for half – price drinks. Back to ours for fun and games with the team.

"Aw, she's all worn out." Let her sleep, you're her best friend from back home remember.

"Yeah well, I'm not waiting around all night I'm going!" Career is good.

By now she was staying almost every night. Each night she was tired and each night she fell asleep. Eventually her friend just assumed she'd be sleeping on the couch and didn't bother to try and wake her. When the door closed behind her, we'd run into the garage and wrap each other up like Christmas presents. Christmas is a time for traditions. Let's put up a tree.

"Yeah, but who invented them?" Deep philosophical debate.

"You talking about Father Christmas' balls?" Mature student.

It was lovely. We made fresh mince pies and drank proper tea from tea pots. We invented new traditions that we could carry on for generations. We couldn't think why we weren't able to. We were fairly sure it wasn't because of God or a baby born in a shed. I made an angel out of tin foil and we put it on the tree.

"We should give her a little kiss before she goes to work." Christmas giggle. Ten times more powerful.

We kissed the little silver angel and our seven-foot-tall Kung Fu housemate Lawrence picked her up so she could place it on the huge real tree my Brother had bought.

"Perfect." Perfect.

The streets were gradually losing the drunken crowds. The students were all going back to see Mum and Dad, Ginger the cat and proud Grandparents. Her best friend from home had gone. Her boyfriend had gone. Her old house was empty.

"Let's have a little goodbye cuddle eh?" Giggle. Shrug. Melt.

"Awwww. I'm gunna miss you, you know." Talk. Pillow.

"Really?" Pupils at precisely the perfect dilation.

I should have kept my mouth shut. Having witnessed all my major fuck-ups by being there and fucking up, I should have known not to sow seeds that might grow into thorns. She had a boyfriend. Was I really that much of a twat? I really was old enough by now to be aware of my actions. The feeling of hopeless desolation I'd felt for so many months was left on the floor with her unfinished essays and cheerleader spankies. Fuck it. I was finally over the sunshine stripper. I felt alive again for the first time in months. I'd been feeling extra festive due to the snow that wouldn't melt for months. I'd been sneaky. I've always loved giving people presents, especially to someone special. My Mini Monroe had expressed more than a curiosity for a little pendant I had around my neck, she wanted it. I told her it was deeply important, that I would be offending Gods if I was to take it off and give it away. She was disappointed. Shit, we don't want to be offending Gods. Not at Christmas. I knew she loved all things 1950s. She was inspired by the art work and design that defined the age, rather than the overt sexism. I found a little book simply titled, '1950's'. Perfect. I pretended, after a drunken mid-week party, that I'd lost my pendant, must have been ripped off in the craze. It was a solid red herring. Sam, my other Kung Fu flatmate had to pick me up and remove me from the house because I'd tried to fight everyone, so the missing pendant deception had legs. I'd drank four litres of Lambrini in just under half an hour, I didn't have legs. I felt a little bit bad when she upturned her student digs in search of my mock religious non-precious artefact but I had a plan. I cut out a small hole in each of the pages of the book, 'Shawshank Redemption' style, minus the mystery murder and the tax, and laid the little red trinket inside the pages. I hoped that she didn't want to read the book after. She squeaked with delight when she unwrapped her pressie. How thoughtful of me. Her squeak turned into a shriek when she opened it. I was dashing through that snow. I was Father Christmas. She jumped on me and we span around. Flopping on the bed I felt cosy. I always felt cosy with her. She was a lovely cup of tea. I was on the 'nice' list for sure.

"I am gunna miss you, you know." Post gift-giving glow.

"Aw, you're gunna miss little me? Why's that?" Monroe coy.

Don't. Say. A. Word. "Because I think …" Shut. Up. "I think that I …" Twat.

"Ooh, it sounds special". Ultra-cute Christmas giggle times a hundred million.

"I think that I …" Arms folded. Shaking my head at myself.

"What you on about Mister?" Share the secrets.

"I think I love you a little bit." Merry Christmas.

"That's okay, cause I'm only little." And a happy new year.

Christmas is a time for family and sharing. Of course I thought the best thing to do next was to offer my festive charm.

"Come and stay with me." Log fires, country house blah blah blah.

"I have to work over Christmas." I do it every year.

"Where you working?" Jobs are for the rest of the year. Surely?

"My mum runs a hotel in the peak district." A whole hotel.

"Does it have a pool?" Turkey and a midnight dip.

"Yeah, wanna come?" A little bit of love never hurt anyone.

We travelled up a windy road to the middle of nowhere.

A majestic old house surrounded by rolling hills with fluffy horses eating frosty hay. She gave us all rooms. We drank cocktails from the bar and I chatted to the residents. Mainly hill walkers and old folk, getting away from the stress and hustle of a political Christmas lunch. We played chess in front of an even bigger log fire and when she'd made the beds and hoovered the rooms she was all mine. Splash. We bobbed and laughed in the heated pool while the snow fell outside in the coldest winter ever.

"What shall we do about your boyfriend?" The love machine cranking itself to full speed.

"I'll have to dump him." Oh no.

"But it's Christmas." Guilt. Twinge.

"He's a big boy." Mistletoe.

When she came back to my room her eyes were puffy.

"You okay, was it bad?" Wow. That was quick.

I felt bad. I dropped the 'love' bomb on her and now she'd dumped her boyfriend from back home. This is what I wanted wasn't it? As much as the excitement of illicit rendezvous made me feel like a cream-slurping cat I knew it was wrong. She'd been crying. I'd made her cry. Who did I think I was? I always used love as an excuse to do irrational things. I'd used love as an excuse for my temper and my selfish desires. I'm shouting at you because I love you. You need to be with me, because I love you. Always wanting to nab the hottest girl around regardless. Why did I need her? Because I loved her, back off, love is powerful, never deny its lure. Always wanting them to fall in love with me so I can drink in the attention and pour my affections over them like hot fudge on a high calorie sundae. This time I felt bad. I'd made this tiny but perfectly formed art student dump her longest ever boyfriend. The one from back home, the one with history. I imagined them having always been a couple. Picking fruit and holding hands together since they were four years old. Shit. I'd turned up, decided I loved her and forced her to break his heart a few days before Father Christmas comes and delivers his iPads. I was a dick. Her face was covered with salty tears.

"No, it's the fucking cat. I love him but I'm allergic." He's so cute and fluffy.

"Oh!" Better get naked then.

My brother and his friends spent the next few nights playing ghost hunters and I spent them curled up with my new girlfriend. Midnight dips in the empty pool. Hungover breakfasts at the staff table.

I rang home to let them know I was bringing a guest to the family home. They were used to an extra setting at the dinner table. Always pleasant and welcoming. Never telling me to stop messing around and just stick with one woman and be happy.

"Bit fucking young for you isn't she?" Stepdad, sage.

"But I love her Rog!" Stepson, onion.

"She better not be another fucking fruit loop veggie." Farmer. Pork.

"She's an artist." She loves tea.

"Artist? Bloody artist." I'll put the kettle on then.

I thought I'd leave out how old she was until we got there. Aliya said that age 'Ain't nothing but a number'. She's dead now, she died young. When I looked at the faces of the girls that were my age, worn out from kids and full-time jobs working for people they hated and doing things they wish they didn't have to, it made me shudder. I'd spent my whole life being told I look young. I'd spent my whole life falling in love with amazing talented beautiful girls. It just so happened that the girl I was currently in love with was only five years old when I started raving in warehouses. So what. Love conquers all. Love builds bridges and love is blind. Love in no way makes you an idiot or takes away any powers of rational thought.

I'd decided to stay on in Leeds for a while longer. I was developing a TV series for a character that got a little sniff from the YouTube community and in turn the tight-trousered beards of Hoxton. I had to develop ideas for my buddy Elskid, and having my own little space in a garage in Leeds with a Kung Fu cheerleader girlfriend seemed like an option I should renew. It was perfect. I'd work while she was in her lectures. We'd train and play in gymnasiums with our action gang in the evenings. We'd potter into the little student village and share the best sandwiches in town. Half for her and half for me. Sharing is caring. We liked exactly the same things. Southern chicken with all the salad, except tomatoes and a little bit of fresh chilli. The only annoying thing was that her now ex-boyfriend was also still her housemate. This made things tricky for her. I half expected him to come and start a bit of trouble, but considering that I was brother to a Kung Fu teacher and living with three other Kung Fu stunt men, I probably wouldn't have come round looking for a fight either.

We had so much fun. She was a sweet cup of tea in a china cup. I loved watching her do her homework, tearing out magazine articles and making scrap books, like the world would really give a shit. We'd sit in parks and play frisbee. Our cheerleader friends would come along and everyone would crowd around and watch as they threw each other in the air while I played cheesy pop songs on someone's acoustic guitar. Occasionally she'd have to go and work for her mum at the hotel. No problem. I'll give her a call to make sure that she's okay.

"You okay darling, what you up to?" Lovely little poppet making her way in the world.

"What do you mean what am I up to?" Long shift.

"Oh nothing, just saying, how's y …" Nope.

"Why are you being like this?" Shouting.

"What? Are you jok …" Oh uh.

"Why are you being such a prick?" Panic.

"Darling I just asked if you were okay!" Bite. Tongue.

"Oh, why don't you just go fuck yourself!" Caller has disconnected.

I literally had no idea what I had done wrong. From past experiences I knew that I didn't always say the right things at the right time but I was fairly sure that I'd just called to see how she was. I thought a little call would make her feel loved and not all alone up there changing dirty bedsheets in rooms full of lavender-water-smelling old-aged walkers. Oh well. Fuck it. She'll be okay when she comes back.

"I just get a bit weird. I don't know why." Giggle. Forgiven. Kissing.

Deal with it. That's what I'll do. I'm older than she is. I've had more experience than she has. I've loved and lost more times than she'd been late for a seminar, which was a lot. No problem at all. Part of me liked her melt downs. She was a miniature Marylyn Monroe with the temper of Tyson. She fascinated me. Her voice was so cute, even when she was telling me to fuck off and die, it was kind of sweet. My friends offered me sage scientific advice.

"Time of the month." Job done.

I'm mature. In a way. I'd dealt with the worst possible case of girl stuff before. There was a pattern. Moon cycles mixed with work cycles and her university deadlines. The cumulative effects of stress and expectation. I'll try and talk, talking is good, I'd learned that. I was in love with a student, surely learning was part of her daily routine. Let's share what I've learned. Now if you can open your books to page one, we can begin.

"You get very angry when you go away darling, is everything ..." Careful.

"Why are you always having a go at me? For FUCK'S SAKE!" Explode.

"Like now, see." Less careful.

"You're always telling me what to do!" Fuck off.

"BECAUSE YOU ACT LIKE A FUCKING BABY!"

Saved by the bell.

In this case the bell was me losing the plot and nothing was actually saved. I'd put up with this behaviour for weeks now. There was literally nothing I could do to help. Everything I said was wrong. Everything I said to her was a well-crafted attack on everything that she held dear. My every breath being an insult to her. I unleashed a torrent of angry facts in her little pretty artistic face. Her sweet tea-loving poppet of a personality cracked and spewed out venom. It was surreal. People didn't believe me when I told them what she'd say to me.

"No, her? Never, she's so cute, must be YOU!" Sigmund Freud.

"She makes me so mad I want to head-butt a lawn mower in the FACE!" Blade side up.

I was furious. How could so much rage come from something that was born from Christmas angels and stolen lips? How could it have transformed into something so stretched out and spiky and mean? I'd told her I wasn't staying forever when I met her. She knew that. Ah. She knew I wasn't staying forever. Flicker of an idea. Guilt. Telling someone you love them is important. It's big. Some people only ever hear it a few times in their lives. The unlucky people never hear it at all.

"I gotta go, the real world's calling me babes." On to the next thing.

"But what about little me?" Who will share my sandwich now?

She'd lost friends and face by moving into my little bedroom with the Kung Fu guys. Her little unit had been ripped apart because she'd decided to fall in love with an older guy who lived in a garage and now he was fucking off and she wasn't in his plan. No one was on her side. I needed to do something grand. A gesture. Something to take her mind away from hating my guts. She was doing a degree in design and fine art. It was time for me to upgrade my laptop, so I decided to give my old one to her. It was a cool silver Macbook that had served me well over the years. I cleaned all the drives and made sure all the software worked for her.

"I wouldn't offer if I didn't mean it." Summer Santa.

"Ooooooh! I LOVE IT!" The giggle was back.

It made me feel nice giving her something that I knew she'd use. Something that would make her life easier and more creative. I watched her little face light up as she booted up the Mac and I watched her little face turn to rage as she pressed play on Recent Videos. Quicktime, you bastard.

"WHAT THE FUCK IS THIS!" Here we go again.

I'd made sure that there were no pictures of my ex-girlfriends on the computer. I didn't want to see them any more than she did. Digital reminders of all the perfect girls that had broken my heart, trash bin.

"Are you sure you want to delete?" Yes, please, and a lobotomy as well if you can Mr Jobs.

I triple checked that all the folders were empty. All traces of any ex-girlfriend were in the electronic wastelands. Fact.

"WHO THE FUCK IS THIS!?" Tiny volcano.

It must have just been in a cache. I honestly hadn't even remembered that the clip was still there. Whoops. My efforts to cheer her up had not gone to plan. Instead of giving her an expensive tool that would help her get amazing grades, I'd handed her a laptop and played her a video of one of my ex-girlfriends dancing semi-naked around a pole. Fucking. Quick. Time.

It took ages to convince her that it was a mistake. I hadn't planned this to fuck her off. I felt so stupid. I also felt for her. She was feeling the tear. We were going to be living hundreds of miles away from each other and to cheer her up I showed her a video of my ex-stripper girlfriend.

"I'm sorry." Genuine.

"I want to burn my eyes out." Genuine.

"I do love you." Genuine.

"Do you have to leave?" Genuine.

"Yes." Genuine.

"Do you want me to come with you when I finish Uni?" Genuine.

"Of course!" Lie.

I just wanted to run. As much as I loved her, I knew that it would never be more then it was. She had a year left of her degree. The world at her feet. I was in my mid-thirties and I'd been playing student for long enough. My Uni buddy Jan was buying a house. Grown-up stuff. Lots of work coming in.

"There's a spare room, cheap rent, you might have to babysit but no bills." Options.

I needed to get back near London. I'd spent nearly a year up North having fun. My little giggler had shown signs of cracking. I wasn't making her happy anymore. One night bliss, the next night hell. Each argument building on the next one. Each tiny mistake or offensive phrase used as ammunition for the next round of insults. It had to stop. I did love her but I knew that if we carried on we'd end up hating each other. That or she'd stab me in the chest while I slept.

• • •

New town, new house. Just me in my little newly decorated bedroom. It had been a few months since I'd seen her. She came to see me on the train. There was an exhibition of one of her favourite artists. Of course we should go. We stood in front of sketches and listened to explanations of genius on little plastic headphones. We walked along the Thames as the sun set over the city. We drank wine and made love for the last time in my tiny brand new room and afterwards I tried to cheer her up as she cried in my arms.

"Why are you giving me this now?" No giggles. Just sobs.

I'd drawn her a postcard. I was going to send it when I left but I didn't. It said how much I loved her and missed her and wished that we could make it work. I thought it would cheer her up. A little reminder of the good times we'd shared. A reminder of everything that we weren't. A written reminder that it was over for good. That she'd never be good enough and that I didn't care. I thought it would be a nice thing. We can laugh about it. The joke would go like this.

1. I'd promise the world.
2. I'd leave town.
3. I'd remind her of all the things we'd never be in a postcard.
4. The girl would see the funny side.

I never heard her little giggle again.

15.

I'd moved back down south to be closer to the action. I had production skills and offers of work. Documentary films, branded content. Head down. Back on target. When the offer to write a rap verse for a hot new female new dance act for my old music pals came I considered it carefully. I'd wasted almost a decade trying to be a pop star. I'd lost the girl I spent so long trying to crack. I'd lost the girl who had thrown away her dreams to make mine an almost reality. I considered it carefully. I considered it for just under three seconds,

"Fuck yeah, I'm on board!" It's only a rap verse. What's the worst that can happen?

Strong Rooms. Trendy Shoreditch. All the skinny jeans, all the facial hair. I'd been away from this world for long enough now for me to see it for what it really was. It's all fake, but fun. Bullshitters bullshitting the bullshit. I couldn't wait to get back in the mix.

"She's a feisty bitch." Friendly warning.

"Let's film our first ever recording session." Always working. Better make an effort.

I'd dressed in my raver's costume. One-piece orange body suit, white fluffy pork pie hat and three dimensional glasses, dancing gloves and pink trainers. The perfect outfit. I thought I was colourful. I thought I was colourful until I met her. Her hair was so red it looked like a super hero space helmet. Intense fringe. Lipstick thick on luscious lips. Pop video body fighting the tiny bikini top under her leather jacket. Teeny tiny hot pants and more gob than Kat Slater. Her smile was so massive that I was glad I had 3D glasses on. At least it gave me a second to gather myself. This girl was impressive. Miles away from being a student, she'd learned everything the hard way and she'd kicked the shit out of it. This was going to be a fun recording session. The song was called 'Take it off'. Cheesy dance tune. Nice.

"Hey, I reckon it might sound better if you get a bit naked in the booth." Long shot.

Boom. She was game. She took off her leather jacket and stood in the hot recording room.

"I'm ready bitches!" Spice girls eat your wigs off.

I joined her. Me rapping my silly verse and her busting shapes. We had to stand next to each other. Headphone cables don't stretch that long. That was my excuse anyway. She was so alive and confident I was instantly on the back foot. Every quip and every cheesy line I spun was met with that headlight grin and a phonetic slap in my balls. It was Intoxicating. After a few hours she went out for some air, leaving me with her equally feisty manager.

"Man she's fucking hot!" Verbal shits.

"You got no chance little raver." Keys to the party.

"It's fine, she's too tall for me anyway." Screw you, management.

Everyone turned to look when she walked in a room. Even Stevie Wonder. Her confidence was as high as her heels and she could sing, she had talent. She was as sure booted as Katy Perry but without the taste of Russell Brand's cock on her bright red lipstick. Her lungs were tasty. I was impressed. All the Spice Girls rolled into one, chuck in a kebab and a bottle of anything and there she was. We drank free bubbles as she signed a recording contract. Immaculate. Her manager told me that I shouldn't bother trying 'it' on as she's just come out of a long term relationship and it's not very professional.

"Maybe she needs a little bit of raver in her life?" Lasers.

Rehearsals were funny. As out of breath as I was, I was surrounded by beautiful talented girls. I appreciated it. I was so far on the wrong side of thirty I knew this was the last time I could be arsed to tart anywhere near the music scene. I was going to enjoy every second. My pop ego returned, this time with no bullshit political questions surrounding my sexuality, the pink pound was as dead as a gay Dodo. I was wearing raver gloves and a sexy super boss was centre stage and she was singing my song. I was in awe of her. I suggested that at one point in the song I should bend each dancer over and pretend to 'do' them from behind. For comedy value. Management considered this. It went in.

She was the star of this project, not me. I was there to add some kind of alluring idiocy. This made me feel so free on stage it was completely new. I didn't care if they were looking at me or not, because if they were they were missing a trick. Neon red hair, skin tight silver body suit, thigh high boots and huge deep purple feathered wings. I was completely transfixed. Professional. Her nerves went from 'oh fuck' to 'fuck yeah' in the beat of a drum. She was magnificent. As she worked the stage, her two dancers beside her writhing and oozing sex appeal with every perfected dance prance, I stole glimpses through my three dimensional glasses. I could hardly breathe. I'd love to say it was my heart exploding with love, but I know part of it was that I was too old and out of shape to be shocking out so hard. Lights, music, dance floor, VIP, free booze, photos. First show over. Let's hit the road.

"Don't shit on your own doorstep." It will end in tears.

I didn't fancy the idea of shitting near anyone's house let alone my own doorstep. I'd been told by more than a few people that trying to get with the main event while on a little UK club tour was a bad idea. What did they know? They didn't know what was going on. Her banter would have destroyed a fleet of white-van-drivers. I just enjoyed flirting. It was adult sexual tension and we were both adults. The heightened state of our own sexuality after thrusting and gyrating on stages in dingy night clubs across the country just made it even sexier. I held out for as long as I could. This being for as long as it took for her to just give in and accept our drunken musical fate. Flopping on her manager's bed after a show and a long drive back to London it was on.

"You're not gunna fuck me, just letting you know." Helpful and informative.

"Thanks, I'm glad I finally got the memo." So. Much. Animal. Tension.

Laying arm in arm with her our bodies were dancing to their own tune. It was unstoppable. It was colourful. It must have looked like two lions dressed in clown clothes having a fight. I say lion. Her manager Nat later told me she thought that there was a walrus in the room having a heart attack. I prefer lions fighting. I felt instantly guilty. Shit, what if this does fuck things up? We're going to have to spend a lot of time together in smelly buses and cheap hotels. I looked down at my latest conquest. That enormous grin, as cheesy as all of my one-liners and lame attempts to get her to fancy me. She was powerful. I realised that I felt like the one being hunted. It was hot. A rapper and a pop singer in bed. We were a low rent version of Kanye and Kim without the arse and the attitude. I felt like a superhero at last. All those years of wishing I could bag a girl like this, independent, creative and driven. She was a star and I was a fan boy. We really shouldn't do this, think of the fall out. Think of the repercussions. We weren't famous. We weren't rich. We really didn't need to make a mess of this project after the first weekend.

"Maybe we should cool it." Big fat liar.

"This will all go wrong." Don't give a shit.

"No, stop if you do that." I won't be able to stop.

"It's fine, I'm not gunna." Stick it in now.

All the weeks of rehearsals, the production meetings the travel and the gigs. All of the little flirty put-downs and the cheeky comebacks. Each one loaded with a deadly concoction of sexual energy, and pure lust rolled into one huge ball and smashed the hell out of us. It was intense. She was strong, I was out of shape. I got bruised. Our teeth clashed, I choked on her red hair, she got angry, we rolled, we laughed, I kicked a fish, we crashed, we sweated buckets. We flopped. Breathe.

"Oh dear…" Oh dear. "Oh dear…" Oh dear.

At least she laughed. She knew exactly what I meant. We'd gone too far. We'd been naughty and ignored the advice of our team. My bravado was brimming.

"Ha, see! I totally did you!" I win.

"Have you seen the state of you?" You're the one who got fucked little man.

Steals the medal.

I didn't care that this would all end in musical tears. I'd finally met my match. She'd beaten me with her wit. She'd beaten me with her performance. She'd beaten me with her body. I lay there battered. We were advised to keep it quiet. Some kind of pop rule. Potential fans won't like it if they think she's involved with a raving idiot.

"Easy." No one needs to know.

Keeping it a secret was fine. I'd played this game before with the girl who giggled. I understood how the whole thing worked. Mum's the word. Smooth sailing from now on.

"You fucking twat!" Firm, but fair?

I had no idea what the fuss was. I did however have a very painful head. It felt as if someone had forced me to drink a bottle of vodka then bang a load of cheap mandy in the bog with a DJ. Yeah. Exactly like that.

"What did I do?" Taylor Swift. Blank space.

According to the team, midway through our last song in an Essex nightclub we'd kissed.

"Aw, nice little peck on the cheek after the last song eh?" Clutching. Straw.

"It looked like you were trying to fuck each other." Stern.

"Well, that's okay? More bang for the buck?" Love is in the air.

"They chucked us out because you jumped off the stage and kicked glasses in everyone's faces." Detail. Accurate.

This was the kind of thing this girl made me do. I wanted to impress her so much I'd do anything stupid to get her attention. I hadn't realised we were on stage at the time, the booze and the apparent drugs altering my reality. All I could see was her futuristic red hair and her laser tits. The best thing about her was that after the initial visual battering, her personality kicked the shit out of you. It kicked the shit out of you with a teenage passion that shouldn't have been residing in a man fast approaching forty.

What made her even more alluring was the attention she got. I'd love to watch the crowds eye her up. I'd see the eager eyes of the drunken punters, I'd overhear their laddish mutterings.

"She'd definitely get it mate." She will if she decides she wants to.

"Tits on that." Are perfectly paid for out of her own money.

"Bet she goes like a freight train." Non-stop to Cairo, you'll need a good rest after.

Seriously, you'll need a rest. I needed a rest. We'd been on the road on and off for a few weeks now. Each venue turning into a blur as I downed vodka to ease my nerves. The old mindset reminding me of all the years I spent trying to get famous while the hardest girl to crack set fire to each of her dreams to make ends meet.

"It's normal, you're both highly charged." Tips from the top.

Our post-show passion had been remixed into something else. Were we boyfriend and girlfriend now? I had no idea. One of our last shows, Wales. I was talking to a girl band from X Factor, they'd narrowly missed out on a place on the live shows.

"Why don't you go and fuck one of them?" Joking. Not joking. Who knows. Not me.

What? This was not the dream. I saw her face. She wasn't impressed. I have to network? I have to schmooze. It's part of the job right?

"I'll just sit in a fucking corner and only talk to blokes then yeah?" Electro logic.

The only other blokes were Stavos Flately and a teenage heartthrob with a guitar. They were headlining the show. Some young kid was absolutely killing it on stage. Handsome, fashionable, eager, hopeful. He was playing acoustic versions of the latest chart toppers and the crowds, mainly girls were going mental for him. I looked down at myself in my stinking rave clobber. I looked up at my dance floor girlfriend not girlfriend. What the fuck was I doing with my life. I'd chased this musical adventure because of her. She'd blown my mind when I first saw her and I'd just been following her around like a puppy on speed. The little tour ended. The track did well. Back to life, back to reality.

Christmas time again. Flying colours. She'd joined in,

chomped the lamb and warmed up by the fires. Maybe this time. Maybe this one would work. I'd tried as hard as I could not to use the love word. I'd learned by now that my Christmas romances never worked out. After the tinsel and repeats of 'Only Fools' had ended the new year stood waiting like a pissed off headmaster.

"If only he applied himself, he'd make a good human being." Scribbly handwriting.

All of my friends were expecting my declarations. She wasn't a silly teenage crush, easily impressed with my flash stories. She was woman enough to know her sexual strengths. She was powerful. She was independent. She was always late. She was in a flap.

"Are you being serious?" Pop Princess.

"Yeah, I'm not fucking about all day waiting for you to do your fucking hair!" Tetchy twat.

"Okay, let's just go then, I'm ready". High heeled wobble.

"Where do you wanna eat?" Resolve.

"Why don't you just fucking decide for once!" Any excuse for a row.

Standing outside the Apple store in central London. All of the nightclub magic and laser light had farted into this. I knew I was being stupid. I could hear myself through muffled filters. It was windy, her immaculate hair was struggling against the bluster. The hair that had hypnotised me before. I could see the look in her eyes. Here we go. I wasn't drunk now.

"Let's just go and eat, you're just hungry." Fact. Hungry for what?

I'd purposely tried not to unleash my proclamations of love. I'd become a joke. No one believed me anymore anyway.

"You can't fall in love so quickly, it's just not real." Everyone an expert.

I sat on the edges and saw all of my friends getting married. Kids popping up on facebook feeds. My timeline becoming a promo for Pampers and Mother Care. Happy faces. Smiling faces.

"I don't even mind getting shit on my fingers, it's beautiful when you think about it." Night caps for nappies.

Time was ticking. For both of us. The biological time bomb tapping its foot, arms crossed, expectant. Our combined age could draw a pension. I knew by now my decisions would ripple and change two futures. Two people who once were strangers. I didn't know if I wanted children anymore. Kids made me face my own mortality. I'd seen the intrinsic value of procreation, I had. They were fascinating. At the end of my days with my sunshine stripper scientist I'd understood the value of it all. A true and unique expression of love between two people. How much more could you show your love for someone than by creating a legacy. A small cuddly wobbly avatar, a perfect mix of Mummy and Daddy. I got it. I understood. This was always bigger than me. I needed to be sensible for once. My dance floor enigma deserved more. We sat in a Thai restaurant on my birthday. We'd been there a few times before. Always giggling over a bottle of wine and the stupid names.

"Kok Bang Soup." One-hundred percent amusing.

The vibe had changed. I know that I'd held back. Chit chats about the future countered with ideals of the present.

"We're still having fun though eh?" Noodles. Uncertainty.

"Are we?" I'll check. Cheque please.

We shot a music video. It was hilarious. Dressed as monkeys we danced and rapped in a mock forest in Ipswich. She looked amazing. The boss. I still adored her. She still impressed me but something wasn't right. She'd been in a long-term relationship just before she signed her deal. He'd been having too much fun on the cunt powder and she'd wanted the limelight over the rolled-up twenty-pound note. I'd come along at the perfect time, a distraction. I latched on to this fact like a coward.

Laying on the bed she told me we needed to have a chat. The old 'chat'. The 'word'. Nothing beautiful ever starts with,

"We need to sit down a have a talk." Nope.

She dumped me. Right there on the bed where we'd played couples over Sykpe. My freeze frame milky volcano still making her laugh. She was gentle and kind. She let me down softly.

"So, yeah, I guess you're dumped." Perfect hair. Perfect smile.

"Hang on, can you say it again while I video it." Hiding behind cameras and stupidity.

Bollocks. I'd let this one slip away. Even after passing the Christmas test. Even after passing the family 'do' test with my crazy cousins and drunken Aunties. My gin-fuelled Mum had dressed up like a zombie to scare her after a heavy night out. She laughed. She got it. She fit right in. Everyone liked her. She was amazing. All these tests. I was single again. Always testing. I was single. All these barriers that I put up to stop me from being happy. Single. Well done me.

We'd milked the ride for as long as we could and we'd had a great time. We'd sang songs in echoey car parks, we'd ran through corridors naked and high on bass lines and booze. We made a dubstep video where I had to get naked and beat her up. It was lovely. My neon star went back to her old boyfriend. The man who had supported her for years as she followed her own dreams. I wondered if I'd told her I was falling in love with her, would it have made a difference? Would it have made me more understanding? Would she have forgiven my impatient and egomaniacal outbursts if we had crossed the border into Love town? Digital gossip. Facebook status update.

"In a relationship." New photos.

Old boyfriend. Happy gallery. Guess I'll never know.

16.

A life-time of broken hearts. A lifetime of judging and comparing. My list was for protection. I knew anyone less would bore me. I was running out of time. I was nearly middle-aged and owned almost nothing. Whereas they had to be …

1. Prettier than Lima.
2. Cooler than Stefani.
3. Kinder than Theresa.
4. Deadlier than Thurman.
5. Brainier than Vorderman.
6. Funkier than Knowles-Carter.
7. More magical than Poppins.
8. Braver than Pankhurst.
9. Ruder than Ozawa.
10. Funnier than Lumley.
11. More awesome than Oswald. And finally …
12. Romantic.

Wow, what a list. What a selfish and pretentious list of things that I hoarded like a teenager with a stolen porno mag. No one would ever be good enough. I was searching for a fantastic idea. I was searching for something that wasn't real and getting older and slower and more selfish every day. I had more and more criteria and less and less to offer.

A lifetime of searching for the 'Perfect Princess' had ended up with me in a small but well decorated bedroom in a town house in Hitchin with my film pal Jan. According to the Telegraph it was the ninth best place to live in the UK, two years in a row. What could be better than that? I wondered what was the eighth. It was a million miles away from my old life. Wandering through the little farmer's markets and dodging the army of suburban yummy mummies. They all looked tired but well dressed and happy. Scores of them sat in leafy parks. Not a man in sight. Probably too busy working long hours playing with numbers in the city to enjoy the rusk covered wobbles and totters of their toddlers. The next generation of taste-makers, factory workers and brides to be. It was old-fashioned and I loved it. I started to knuckle down. The offers of jobs turned into money in the bank. The money in the bank allowed me to be creative again. In the space of a couple of months I was firing on all cylinders. My best friends all having babies around me. Getting married. Beginning legacies and bloodlines that would tell tales of how they met for generations to come. I started to think I'd got it all wrong. I started to think that I'd missed the boat.

"They'll be yachts, dolphins and all kinds of cool shit!" Low pay but high seas and lavish times.

"Fuck yes!" When do we leave.

Different kind of boat, but I'm not missing this. My film buddy Robin had landed a dream job. Months and months of filming in the Indian Ocean for a hotel brand. Maybe I hadn't missed the boat after all. Fuck this romance shit. Fuck falling in love. I'd tried to convince myself, year after year, decade after decade that love was the most important thing in the world. Nothing can be bad when you're in love. All those happy couples in Sudan and Fukushima, loving each other in bliss while I cried about the ideal woman I could never find. The one who would listen to all of my insane rhetoric and excuses not to join in and just settle the fuck down.

I had to laugh. I had to laugh hard and loud. Our mission for the next few months was to film five-star hotels. Each and every one full of passionate rich couples, wedding parties, honeymooners and gold anniversary diners illuminated by the light of the setting sun. I was in the most romantic place on Earth and I was with a man who had just had a gorgeous baby with a beautiful dancer. The universe was pulling down my Tom Baker shorts and shoving a pineapple up my arsehole. At least it was fresh. The pineapple that is.

In my pursuit of perfect romance, I'd come up short. Either I got bored or decided that she wasn't good enough. Mean. Stupid Eighties teen movie ideals, I was the chump not the anti-hero. After a long day's filming I stood up to my waist in crystal clear warm water and looked out to sea. I couldn't tell where the water ended and the sky began. A mirrored canvas spanning for the whole of eternity. Pinks, yellows, reds, blues, greens. Gold and silver beams ringing invisible church bells that lived in my head. It was the single most beautiful thing I have ever witnessed. I wished that I could have shared it with someone. Someone special. Well, someone other than Robin who was getting pumped up about a ping pong rematch.

"Yeah big wow, fucking sunset, get the ball. Loser's a cunt!" Forehand technician.

We played a lot. The job was lucrative. For the first time in my life I wasn't worried about making the next rent cheque. I wasn't even worried about sauce. My food was just as tasty without it. It was a strange feeling. I'd given up on the idea of love and finding someone. I subconsciously handed over the gene torch to my younger brother. I'd be a great uncle. I was already a Godfather. My now eighteen-year-old Godson Matthew being my finest vicarious creation. He liked electronic music, video games and hot babes. My work was done. Easy-peasie, half-Chinesie. I had money in my pocket and my heart wasn't falling or broken. A stale state of 'tried my best' mixed with 'not quite good enough'. Buying trousers and vintage Star Wars figures replaced my thirst for true love.

Being the eldest son of the eldest son, my Eastern family were concerned. I'd batted off Oriental heat for the last twenty-five years. Each Auntie telling me to stop dreaming and get a proper job. At my Dad's 60th birthday party my brother and I flew out to Hong Kong to revel in the free twelve course meal.

"Why you no marry?" Prawn breath.

"Need to find a nicee wifee!" Getting old now.

"Better make for baby is good." Where's our grandson you fucking idiot?

Irony. My English family were only ever concerned for my happiness. My Chinese counterparts couldn't give a shit what I did as long as I got hitched. Trying to explain to them I'd been trying my hardest since the age of eight was like shooting rabbits in a pond with a cream bun. They just didn't get it. I consoled myself with the elicit professional services hidden away from embarrassed eyes on main roads with huge neon signs and exotic women wearing chong sums in the doorways shouting best prices.

"Mister like pretty girl now?" Thirty minutes left.

"Yep, bring her in." I wondered if I'll just cry as she finished me off?

"You got girlfriend back home?" Standard patter.

"Au m'hai loi pang yau." She won't see me cry, it's dark in here anyway.

We'd managed to scrape enough work to afford a little office above a charity shop. 'Buzz Films' and 'Super Massive', short films and music videos. We filled it with shelves full of kit and white boards full of ideas. My mind was busy. I had no time to think about getting old or being lonely. Things were starting to go the right way. My mind was free to focus on what mattered. Being creative. Generating leads. Making money. I'd always had a strange relationship with money. I never cared about it as long as I was balls deep in the whirlwind of romance. Having been single for a while I was lonely I knew this, but relatively loaded. Money was my mistress. The office was my playground. We'd smash out video treatments until we got peckish. I loved having lunch. Lunch was good. Posh lunches were even better. Lunch was what she suggested when she messaged me, out of the blue.

"What the fuck is chocolate ganache?" I want a McFlurry.

Sat in a Cafe Rouge, my heart was thumping. Lunch time head fuck. My chest was beating so hard I thought that the cheesy jazz they were playing had been tampered with by a YouTube remasher. My mouth was dry. This was going to end badly. I knew for a fact that this was the worst idea that I could ever think of. Twenty-one years old and a single mum. Two-year-old daughter whisked off to her Grandma's for the afternoon. None of these things screamed 'plain sailing' or 'easy street'.

"Just looks like a posh Mars Bar." Honest to a fault. Actually correct.

She was a blast from the past. I'd known her through my old band life. She was a talented young teenage dancer with all the stages at her feet. Her attitude was hip hop. Her look was anime. Her huge brown eyes were equally full of sadness and the most exquisite beauty, all rolled up with a middle finger to the world. I was in trouble. Red alert. Run away. For God's sake, RUN!

"But she's got a kid." Surely this will have made her mature. Grow up.

The age gap was big. But the words of the dead R&B singer rattled through my head. Maybe age is just a number. It wasn't unheard of. My cousin Emma married a guy almost twenty years older than she was and they did it in Vegas. They were perfect for each other. He was

cool, she was happy. Why not us? Having to face a world
of nappies and bottles and late night grumbles must have
steered her into a more thoughtful mindset? When I'd
known her before she was experimenting. The streets
were her laboratory and she was on fire. Every boy, man,
club owner, mechanic, hoodlum or chicken shop delivery
guy would falter in her loud and manic wake. I loved it,
she was exciting. I was pleased for her. Why not? Taste
the delights of the world before you knuckle down and
become the next dance sensation. She was a pussy cat doll.
She was going to be the next big thing. Now she was a
young mum. She worked at a care home helping old folk
smile in their last days. No more dancing. No more shows.
No one reliable for her daughter to call Daddy.

"You can come round to mine for dinner if you want."
Babysitter.

"Yeah, okay I'll cook us a surprise." Sophistication.

"I don't have much stuff in." Small kitchen.

"That's cool, I'll bring food, you got pots and pans and
stuff yeah?" Just checking.

"Duh, of course I have, I'm not a fucking moron you
dick." All the single ladies, independent.

I bought around a bag of shopping. I wanted to show
off my culinary skills.

"What the fuck is a spatula?" Made-up words make
me laugh.

I was always good at improvising. This young woman
had seen my eager attempts at pop stardom. My escapades
filtered through teenage shades. Now it was different. She
laughed at my vanishing six pack. She took the piss at every

possible step. She made me laugh. She was wise beyond her years when it came to the things that she saw, the things that she found funny. She told me I was up my own arse and I knew she was telling the truth. She told me about her daughter's dad being a knob. Falling pregnant early and making big decisions. I could hear my twisted steed neighing and huffing in the distance. My sword and shield being dragged out and wiped free of cobwebs. She was a damsel in distress. I had the time and the money. I wanted to buy a horse and take riding lessons so I could rescue her. This was in no way a good idea. Even she agreed.

"This will all end in tears, you doughnut." True.

"Nah I'm a big boy now." True.

"You're an old man now." True.

"At least I know what a spatula is darling." True

"You're a wiener." True.

"I'm worried you're going to fall in love with me." True

"I'm done with that shit." Lie.

I'd used an Argos catalogue as a chopping board and a Dora the Explorer knife to cut the veg. I mixed the salad dressing in a Peppa Pig cup. I set the little table with a candle. Sophistication. It was heady, it was loaded. The smile on my face was worthy of a Cheshire cat. We ate our meal and drank wine listening to Kiss FM on her huge TV. When we'd finished she leaned out of the window and smoked a cigarette. Just the two of us. Her little girl was with the Granny. Before when I knew her she was a feisty teenage rebel. Covered in all the makeup. Gob as quick as her dance moves, orange tan and false shiny bright teeth. She hadn't changed much. She was still gobby.

"You're a bit fat now innit." Poke.

"I want to see you without all the camouflage." Little bit brave.

"Never in a million years." My armour is staying.

Every atom in my body wanted her. Naturally beautiful under all the slap. She reminded me of Chun Li from street fighter, but with a better arse. Buns of steel, Chun Buns. She was a real life anime girl. Her sass and self-assuredness were as much a mask as her 'St Tropez'. I wanted to see her.

"Take the hair out at least." I dare you.

"Fuck off, I'm going for a piss." No chance.

I laughed. She pushed past me and I felt her hand linger on my waist. I knew it was on. We were alone in the house, the washing up was done. The wine bottles were empty. When she came back she was fresh-faced. Hair a mess after ripping out extensions. Sexy new outfit replaced by a dressing gown. Make-up gone. I'd never seen anyone so pretty in my life.

"I'm not taking my eye lashes off so deal with it." Clean. Beautiful. Mine.

I didn't care that she still had inch long lashes. The fact that she'd shed her outer layer meant more to me than it should have done. I felt as if she was letting me in. Letting me see her for who she really was. A young woman with dreams of dancing all over the world who made a choice and stuck by it. She kissed me in the kitchen. A single perfect kiss.

"Shall I sleep on the sofa tonight?" Just checking.

"Yeah, I'll get you a blanket." Straight-faced.

"Ah, that's, erm, cool then I'll just ..." Flustered.

"You're still such a loser." Grab. Pull. Bedroom. Boom.

Sat on the bus on the way back home I made a promise to myself. Whatever happens I was never going to fall in love again. I was doing good, making money and paying my bills. This is what grownups should be doing. Not playing Mills and Boon with any beautiful girl that dared to catch my eye. Not even with my Chun Buns fantasy single mum. I'd learned by now that all that will follow will be pain and suffering. Each trip to love central watched over by the Emperor, shooting dark lightning into my underwear. Besides, I'd have to find another park and get my running shoes out.

I'd met her years before when she was a dancer. A fun little theatre academy run by the craziest couple you'll ever meet. They were romantic. They'd been together for twenty-five years and fooled us all with a surprise wedding on the secret bride's fiftieth birthday. They understood my romantic flights of fancy, they'd seen me fall and they'd picked me up. I confided in James their ten-year-old son.

"I think she's scared to been seen with me in town in case her family finds out." He got me.

"Start dance class again, then you can hang out with her and they'll never know?" Young Wisdom.

I suggested this to my real life lady Street Fighter. It was perfect. It wasn't unusual for me to take Zumba or Street Dance. I'd spent thousands of hours shaking my ageing body in front of ceiling-high mirrors. In fact, it would be more suspicious if I didn't go. Great plan. Ten years old and already cleverer than I was. We'd both arrive, minutes apart.

"Oh, I didn't know you were still coming here." Nosey parkers.

"Yeah, how fucking odd!" Wink wink.

Julia, the dance master sussed within the count of eight.

"She'll mess with your brain." Motherly concern.

"I know what I'm doing, just a bit of fun." Bare faced. Silly boy.

We'd meet in the stolen hours between Grandma's house and Nursery. She'd arrive in her massive Jeep and we'd saunter to places out of the reach of gossipy eyes and tell-tale tongues. She let me take her hand as we walked through Hitchin town. It was almost Christmas again. Festive. Time for buying gifts for those we love.

"Aw look, it's got her name on it!" Wicker picnic basket. Embroidered text.

As we walked around the little brick-a-brac shop we laughed at the tat and we 'ooooh'd' at the treasures. There were some kitchen utensils there. I held up a large yellow cheese grater.

"Oh, they have spatulas!" Funny.

"You're not funny." I fucking am.

I asked the lady behind the counter to save the picnic basket with her daughter's name while my real life Chun Li wasn't looking. I wanted it to be a nice surprise. Inside were tiny little cups and saucers made out of real china. So delicate. I imagined that when the summer came we could all go to the park by the river and have her little girl's very first proper picnic. I'd tell her all about where tea comes from. The huge mountains of Peejee Tips, where the leaves are hand-picked by well-trained Indian monkeys with bandanas. You can't beat a picnic by the river with real china cups, even if you are only two and half years old. Shit, I was making plans. I was making plans without first consulting anyone or even giving a toss.

"You'll have to meet her first." With one, comes the other.

I was looking forward to it. A little tiny version of her anime mama. I admired how she took the responsibility on. She was a single mum, barely out of college. She was worried what she'd say. Toddlers are great at being honest.

"Want Mummy's friend to read me a story again." The one with the picnic basket?

Must be imagining things. Kids talk crap. That was her only angle on the whole situation. Worried that her family would find out about her illicit rendezvous with a much older guy. A guy that by now should have his own toddler. Spending Sundays making up for lost time and nodding politely at the other dads by the swings. What was wrong with him? Why was he hanging around with a single mum. What the hell did he want? I just wanted to make her life perfect. I wanted to let her know that she was still talented. That she still had the world at her dancing feet. I wanted to make her feel safe in her little flat and not panic when she heard the downstairs door shudder and clang. I wanted to whisk her away with her little mini Chun Buns and live in a dream world of stories and picnics and kissing. The normal stuff. Realistic things. Had I consulted her about all these plans? Of course not, they just whirled around in my head like a loved up bee, filling my brains with honey. I'd already been at her flat for an hour or so.

"I'm gunna pick her up." And we're off.

I waited at her flat for the sounds of toddling. Nervous. I knew most kids liked me. I think's it's because a two-and-a-half-year old has about the same amount of sense as I do. Oh look a balloon! My hands were damp and my mouth was dry. I'd never been so scared to meet someone so tiny. In my mind the whole future of me and my real life Chun Li rested on two facts.

1. Will she like me?

2. Will she blab to her Grandparents?

"Don't kiss me in front of her, she's got a gob on her." Like Mother. Like Daughter.

Crash. Footsteps. Pitter patter. Bash and clatter. A mini hurricane of pink and flashing lights burst into the room. She threw her little bag on the settee and started to spin, she laughed and laughed and span faster and faster.

"You'll fall over silly moo." Mum knows best.

"No I won't Mummy! I'm a princess!" She fell.

More laughs. More giggles. She was adorable. A perfect version of her beautiful mother. Dark hair and dark eyes, olive skin and the cheekiest grin I'd ever seen. Fuck. She looked a bit like me. If I hadn't known she wasn't mine, I'd have put money on the fact that she was. It was scary. I'd never really been so face to face with the prospect of my own child. I'd talked about it with the sunshine stripper, but she was curly blonde with green eyes, who knew what strange mutation would have popped out. This little girl in front of me was the perfect version of the child I'd always had in mind. The hair, the eyes, the infectious laugh and spinning around until she fell over with a bump.

"I fell over!" Which is HILARIOUS. "Again!" Orders from the top.

"You little nutter!" Picked up. Spun round. Dumped on the settee with a whomp.

I instantly fell in love with the idea that this could all be mine. I instantly forgot that:

1. She wasn't my child.

2. She didn't need another Dad.

3. It would be a large ball ache for Mummy.

I didn't care. The love monster had risen. That romantic monster who smashes down walls to show its truth. A monster who feeds on what ifs and maybes. A monster that couldn't give a shit about repercuss ... I won't even finish the word. Who cares what nightmare will ensue, as long as there's love in the air. All the things that really matter, suddenly don't. Sat in a small flat off a bust main road I had a tiny cartoon child on my lap. Her beautiful mother sat by my side, making sure she was careful not to get too close. A little wiggle of her toe telling me it's okay.

"She wants a story." Test number one.

I'd never been so happy in my life. Having kids is easy. That's what I like to tell my friends who are on week thirty of seventy-five minutes of sleep a night. They love it. How hard can it be? Make the rules up as you go, you're the parent now, if it was so hard how come all these people on Jeremy Kyle can have so many? Plus, they always look so fresh on that show and so full of passion. Passion is good. I took a deep breath. I felt like this was the defining moment of my life. If I got this right, she'd fall in love with me, ring up her dad and tell her that she's getting married to a man fifteen years older than her who makes videos about Mauritian hamburgers for a living. Simple. The little pink bundle clambered over me and plonked herself on my lap. She snuggled into me and when she was sure that I was comfortable enough for her she looked up at me, expectant. Here goes.

"Once upon a time…" Safe start. Shit, drawing a blank here.

"In a galaxy far, far away…" Okay, getting somewhere.

I needed to set the scene but I needed characters, no story is worth a shit if there are no people involved.

"There was a boy called … LUKE!" Hell yes.

My obsessive fascination with Star Wars had finally paid off. Ha! All those people who said I was an idiot paying nearly three hundred quid for a vintage figure can all suck my plastic. I was on fire. Her brown eyes lit up when I described the Princess.

"She's like your Mummy, she was the most beautiful and cleverest Princess in the galaxy." No, she doesn't live in a bar of chocolate. Why can't she?

By the time the Death Star had exploded we'd bonded through laser swords and hairy dog slaves. I was waiting for the nightmare loop of,

"Again, more, again, again!" Feed my brain.

I had Empire Strikes Back in my pocket, I was ready for anything, but no. She was sated. Her little girl closed her eyes and curled into a warm wiggly ball and let out a little sigh. Her Mum seized the opportunity and gave me my report card. Gently placing her hand over her daughter's sleepy eyes, just in case, she leaned over and kissed me. A warm, loving kiss. Better to be safe than sorry though eh?

"Hey! I can't see mummy!" Cheeky laugh. Everything's a game.

Everything was a game. Winners and losers. Sat on a settee with a happy child and a happy Mother, in that instant, I felt like I'd won all the lotteries. I had the winning ticket. Better phone the newspaper. I want a photo of me with a massive cardboard cheque.

"Oh, hey, what are you guys doing for Christmas?" All the trimmings. One last shot. No pressure.

I promised the same deal as always. Country house. Fireplace. Cats. Roast potatoes and cocktails. Her eyes lit up. Escape. That's what she wanted. That's what I could give her. I imagined the faces of my family as I turned up in her big off-road truck, a perfect readymade family. Entertaining and confident offspring. Beautiful young woman. Me. Smug. Family the shit out of it. The goose was getting fat.

"I'll have to tell my Dad we're just friends though innit." Too much too soon.

I didn't care about her Dad. So what if I was way too old for her. He'd have to get used to it. I was a grown man with my own opinions and ideas. I'd done things, see things and had my fair share of knuckle and feet sarnies. I wasn't scared one bit.

"Shit!" Shit.

"What?" Shit.

"My Dad's here." Shit.

"Hide in the bedroom!" Shit.

"Now?" Shit.

"Now!" Shit.

"Shit." Yes, shit.

I'd stayed over at her little flat. Her daughter was at her sister's house. Young mum, and a young auntie. They were twins. I knew that the Father and Daughter relationship was tense. All the promise, all the pregnant promise. He must have loved her, but they are always at each other's throats. Ah, throats. I kind of need my throat for breathing. I ran into the bedroom and she pushed me under the bed near the window, the furthest place from the door. Keep. Still. Don't breathe.

"He would have so killed you!" Not a pork pie in sight.

"Ha, well, he didn't scare me at all." Close call.

"Then why did you shit your pants and run into my room like a wiener?" Observational.

I tried to laugh it off. My confidence slipping. This was going to be hard. She was a single mum with a spiky relationship with her father. I was a single man with a spiky relationship with reality.

"I'm going to town; my sis has her till tonight." Declare. Not invite.

She was going to meet up with some friends at the

big shopping centre in town. Her sister was looking after her daughter until later that evening so she seized the opportunity to be just herself for a few hours. Twenty-one years old. Twenty-one minutes to herself.

"I'll come with you." Let's hold hands and skip and laugh and dance wearing silly jumpers.

"Nah, meeting my mates, I can't be seen with you." Right in Santa's sack.

I knew that this was all supposed to be hush hush. I knew that we'd been living some illicit festive daydream that was fuelled by an enduring physical attraction. I wanted to tell her I loved her. She wanted to get a bargain from H&M to wear when she was allowed out for the night. We kissed and went our almost separate ways. This was just a hurdle. I knew this was going to be tricky. I convinced myself that love as always would prevail and find the solution. Hiding the lies and the torment under dilated pupils and porn star sauce.

I was peckish. I knew where she'd be. I told myself that I really, really wanted a pretzel from the shopping centre. I really really wanted one. Especially as they were four quid and took ages to make. I spent the next ten or so minutes walking up and down the tinsel lined marble halls. I walked past it more than once. I walked past it until I saw her. With her friends. Arms linked. Laughing. Taking the piss. The things normal twenty-one-year old girls do. We locked eyes. A donkey kicked me in the chest. Ha. Finally, she'd have to acknowledge me now. Our eyes unlocked just as fast. Her friends looked at me like I'd just had a shit on a nativity scene then sang a Bollywood number wearing a hijab. She turned away. There it was. Right there. Reality. What was I doing? When she turned away it felt like lightning in my guts. I watched as she melted into the Christmas crowds. Standing there like a cheesy pretzel. With a cheesy pretzel. Ho Ho Humbug.

All of a sudden the texts went from a hundred a day to one. She used to call me from her new job, sometimes she'd tell me, "I'm hiding in a cupboard". So truant. She'd ring and tell me about her day. She'd unload the politics of a proper job into my freelance ears. I loved it. I felt like I was helping. I felt like I had the key to making her life perfect. It never occurred to me that her friends, her family or her daughter's father may have something to say about all this. I knew that he was a good-looking guy. Her daughter, as much as I thought she looked like my own child was a mix of the two of them. She was stunningly cute. All I knew, was that he was a looker, did a bit of sport but didn't want the responsibility.

"Is that her Dad?" Facebook hell. "No that's erm ..." Suddenly coy.

"That's erm?" The tease of temper and nausea. "It's fine, I'm a grown up, is he a mate or something?" I have tons of girl buddies, I'm down with gender equality, I've seen the Hemline Index three times.

Just some guy she knew from around the town. He was good to her when she first left her daughter's father. Nice. I like a man who is there for his friends. Especially when there's a little life involved. Commendable.

"Ever been to Winter Wonderland?" A ram-packed cattle market of tat and tourists. Perfect.

"Nah, is it good?" Window. Cigarette.

"We should go together; I'll treat you both." Spreading cheer like goose fat.

I was excited. I imagined taking the tiny bundle on her first carousel as I held her young mother's hand under the millions of fairy lights. We'd walk through the crowds and everyone would 'ooh' and 'ahh' at our beautiful trio. Japanese tourists would stop us and ask for our picture. They'd laugh with Nippon embarrassment but walk away with pride at meeting such a fabulous family unit.

"Can't get a babysitter." Flat.

"What about Sunday?" Mistletoe and wine.

"I've got her all weekend." Duty calls.

Babysitters. A world that I would have to get used to. Having a toddler is tough especially when you're living by yourself. I was disappointed when I found out that we couldn't go to Winter Wonderland. Part of me was revelling in the fact that the whole thing was in Hyde Park. When I stayed with my sunshine stripper scientist we would watch the crowds grow and the lights shine from her living room window high up in the Knightsbridge sky. I was fairly disappointed that we wouldn't be going. I was fucking furious when I saw the pictures online.

The carousel was there. The gorgeous toddler and the beautiful young mum were there. The so-called 'just a friend' was there too. Smiling. The three of them. The Essex boy Grinch that stole my perfect Christmas season. Jingle bollocks. Jingle bollocks all the way.

"Babysitter my arse!" Confusion. Temper.

"Look, I'll come and see you in a few days." Diffusion

She told me that she'd be in the car park at lunchtime. I sat in my small well-decorated room and watched for her silly big car. I sat and I waited and waited. I sat not moving, eyes on the road. Before she'd call and I'd be sat next to her within twenty- five minutes in the car park across the road. It was immediate. It was fast. It was Maccy Dee's.

"Share a McFlurry?" And a snog in the four by four.

I gave in when it was dinnertime. We spoke the next day on the phone. I shouted at her. My fuse blown from a Wonderland snubbing. I told her she was a bitch for lying to me and that I hated her. Nothing beautiful ever began with the words, 'We need to talk'. Nothing beautiful ever ended with the word's 'Bitch', 'Lying' and 'Hate'.

I spent Christmas without the eye candy on my arm and the bag of chuckles on my knee. No romantic fireplace snuggles and no special presents under the twinkly tree. No sarcastic well-meant chit chat over the roast lamb about my latest festive squeeze. No hope of the perfect romance arriving via the chimney wrapped with a bow. New Year's eve came and went. I spent it with my friend Jay watching videos of nerds getting violent revenge on bullies and skateboarding videos from the Eighties. It was different.

"You don't want another man's fucking offspring." Jan made sense.

"But she was so cute, she wanted to listen to my stories." I do love Star Wars.

"You'd have to kill it and eat it, like lions do." My brother made sense.

Winter turned to Spring and love was in the air, just

not mine. My well-decorated room was now part of a
house with a shiny new couple. Things got gooseberry
and I got out. I kept myself busy with work. Our little
office above the charity shop was churning out good
ideas but I was bored. Bored of it all. I had decided to
give up my life-long search for the impossible Princess, I
needed to do something different. I needed something, not
someone new. Something that didn't involve women and
my headless pursuit. I felt like a broken Valentine's day
yoyo. A shambolic miserable libertine.

"We're going out and you're cheering the fuck up!"
Oxford intent.

Robin and I went for a last drink while his wife and
newborn were away at her Mum's. The ninth best place
to live in England was full of affluent charismatic single
women and I didn't see one of them. They all blurred into
some kind of living hormonal judging panel. Looking
down their noses at me with my sack full of woe as I
ordered my tenth desperado. I couldn't be bothered at
all. I had nothing to say. Zero. The flirty young men and
professional suburban hipsters flaunting their magazine
beards and slick-back trousers. Working hard to catch the
eye of the peahens in their new look. They all made me
want to start a fight, chuck a chair through a window and
vomit. In that order.

Half running away and half being brave, I'd decided
to up sticks and leave for the lights of London town. This
time, my plans were to become the world's greatest actor
in a single year. Ambitious. A little bit of me had always
hoped that the girl in the black and white photo would

have seen me one day on Top of the Pops and forgiven me for all the shitty things I did and said to her. The only trouble with that scenario was my band fell apart, they cancelled Top of the Pops and she married a professional footballer. I knew years ago that was never going to happen and I was okay with it. I'd gone from one girl to the next and each one had ended. I still had no idea why?

"Stop telling them you love them after a week you fucking twat." Wisdom of a first-time Dad.

Life in London was fast. I made friends with a guy called Eric, well-connected and camp as shandy. We zipped and zapped from West-end show to Chipotle margaritas and I found my feet in an acting class. My amazing new mentors told me to focus. If I wanted to act, if I wanted to be in EastEnders as a Chinese bad guy, I'd have to stop all this messing around. Stop the cycle of falling and breaking. Being in love wasn't the most important thing in the world, it was just one of them. A good thing, but not the only thing. I lost myself in the class, Meisner. A weird mix of voodoo and drama. Unlocking truths and demons that only just hid about under the surface. It was magnificent. It was challenging. I fucking loved it.

Everywhere I went I was surrounded by beautiful people. In every casting all the girls were at their very best. Smiling at anyone in case they held the pen that ticked the box. Fake but amusing. There were so many gorgeous women I forgot all about being in love. I forgot all about the concrete javelin in the spleen that always follows the same old fall. I was single. I was learning. I was happy. I considered telling my mum that she'd be waiting a long time for her little granddaughter. I'd missed the love boat but I was sailing just fine by myself. I'd be the new landlord of the Queen Vic in a matter of months. I didn't have time for all that gooey stuff anyway, I'd be way too busy charming the support pants off the Loose Women and being 'Torso of the week' in Heat magazine.

17.

I had met her before, twice to be almost precise. Platinum cropped hair and tattoos on her feet. The first time was in an empty freezing BBC TV studio, where they used to film Dr Who in the sixties. It was a Meisner acting session and she'd come to try out the class, brave, as it's a fucking weird way to spend five hours.

Her fearlessness made her even more interesting than her Canadian swagger. I was transfixed, I was amused, I shit my pants. We went for a drink after, a little pub in Marylebone with a tall bombshell of an actress called Rose and a groovy classmate called Bill. The place was nice and posh, the usual London arsewipes. Lots of perfect hair, skinny clothes and ironic bollocks. Only this time I wasn't thinking about murdering the myriads of graphic designers with their posh half good-looking pregnant wives as they mock argue about what finish to have on the second Eco kitchen as I panic over choosing to quit directing films and making money to follow my passion to become an actor.

I was, instead, listening to a barrage of tales far more interesting than recycled tiles, loaded with such kudos I felt like a fat ginger kid at a new school. Each tale telling me its own story but part of one much more important. The Canadian's story. I looked and listened to her like she was that extra half hour of TV before bed. I didn't care what was on, I just wanted to watch it. In a flash I was walking to the tube, I felt dizzy, most likely the five-hour cry fest that we call 'the work' and the two pints of Guinness, but a small part of me knew it was the Canadian and a smaller part of me thought, this girl is trouble.

The second time I met her I had been invited to drinks with my new acting agent, I'd just been signed to a mid-level agency after a show I did in Leicester Square, one night only but it was still the to the West End so, I was quite pleased. The night started badly. My agent Tom left a text, I called him, his phone was dying. They were moving on to ... then nothing. Stranded in trendy Shoreditch with a pocket full of money and no one to hang with I remembered that my amazing friend Rose, who lives on a boat on the Thames, worked at The Rivington. Nearby, great steaks. Bingo! I'll go and see what's going on, see my acting buddy and try and blag some free food.

Sat at the bar tucking into some amazing nosh, I made a friend, an American. Rich, friendly and stupid. I liked him straight away. We chatted crap and drank booze until Rose finished her shift and we hatched a plan. The American wanted to party hard. Harder than tequila and a lot scratchier on the nostrils. I've been out of the drug scene for years now, my rave days happily sitting in the Nineties, so I drew a blank, but the Canadian had things "covered". Wow! There'd been a class A throw down and I hadn't even noticed. I was either too slow or in the presence of something exciting. Even as I crashed towards forty, I knew for a fact I'm not slow. This, was definitely exciting.

I was in a montage. Guy Ritchie was pulling the strings, but the Canadian was the leading lady. Dark noisy bars which minutes ago were 'full mate, sorry' were suddenly 'open, come on in'. She had the trendiest street in London dancing to her song. This girl was rock and roll. I remember more drinks, and singing Stevie Wonder in a flat with a bath in the bedroom and in another flash I was in a cab with a lovely Indian guy who'd actually rang me at four-thirty AM and wondered if I needed a lift home. The universe was smiling, but this girl was almost certainly trouble.

The next time I met the Canadian it took me by surprise. I had been to see Rose's new play, 'The Hemline Index' at a little theatre and had just caught a glimpse of her before the lights went out. Giddy with pride for my theatrical compadre my attention was being pulled in a totally unexpected direction. This direction mainly involving the Canadian playing piano and dropping rap bombs wearing platform heels and the sexiest little outfit I'd ever seen. I really dug it. I had heard her sing once before, powdered up after a hard night's work and as much as she tried that time, it's hard to sing when you're wasted, trust me. I used to be in a pop band and getting wasted was the only thing that made it fun. That and sauce with dancers. This time around it was different. Something about her had changed. Her intentions, hidden so deeply behind her changing eyes had a new conviction. Fuck knows what it was but it demanded my attention. This girl was fascinating, this girl was funny, this girl was genuinely cool. As the barman begged with tired eyes – 'please fuck off' – we needed a cab. A small group of us left, full of pride and drink and we clambered into a minivan. The Canadian and I ended up in the back. As we slipped and slid in the boot to full voice verses of Pulp I thought to myself, this is the best cab ever, the driver's so nice, letting us choose songs and do backflips. Ironic really that as a result of her drunkenness mistakenly stole the driver's belongings, but it was sorted out by a responsible adult. After some pizza and a smoke, I found myself in bed with the Canadian and Rose, which sounds much sexier than it was, Rose being an immovable beauty and the former being a sniffling crumb ridden fidgety squirrel. The cold hard floor rather than a hot hard threesome seemed the most ideal solution.

As the sun screamed "get the fuck out of the flat!" I was off. Rose had promised me a tour and I had nothing else to do. The Canadian was battered, she half-muttered something about hair and dye but I wanted to go. After all, I mainly thought this girl was, you know, trouble, and I mainly wanted to shoot for a trouble-free-zen-like existence, finally freeing myself from the curse of infatuation and dream girl fantasy. Mumbling 'I wanna hang with you guys' she went back to sleep and Rose and I hotfooted it to the high seas, via Canary Wharf.

It was hot. A real summer's day. Not even a freaky blip. Summer sun. The whole of London had sunburned forearms and their feet in Diana's wet circle. Rose had lost her key so we had to climb through the kitchen window. Melting chocolate and warm white wine fuelled our decadence as we bobbed gently on the River Thames slowly going nowhere. The muddled daydream of the hangover that wants to be drunk again was woken by the sound of a platinum-haired filmmaking singing waitress who looked like she was going to be sick.

"Sup bitches, like fucking yo, yo!" Accent. Wobble. Beer can.

No thanks. Not now. I was having a lovely time bobbing with my new nautical best friend. We were about to listen to Lana Del Ray and talk about how awesome she is. I didn't want this health warning poster girl to puke on me. That probably sounds a little harsh, but I was just being precautionary and besides, this girl is trouble right?

Well, no. Maybe not. Uh oh. I had a weird thought. Maybe she wasn't so much trouble after all. Wanker. Before I had even realised I'd spoken, I'd offered to make her dinner. Punch me now. I gave her my usual cheesy bullshit about cooking her a fantastic meal.

"Course it's all fresh, my Dad cooked for Neil Armstrong." Space bloke.

She can take refuge and absorb the good vibes of our home and revitalise her ebbing lust for life. She was transient, travelling, she'd hit London hard, and recently it hit her back even harder. This time though my cheese felt a little sincerer, my fromage had matured. Her turn of phrase filled me with such intrigue I just wanted to laugh and be impressed at everything she said, until now I never knew that guacamole needed 'centralizing', but when I thought about it, like her, it seemed to make sense.

After a while as the clock tocked on I thought, do I really need to cart a drunken, shakey, drugged-up Canadian back to my home? My secret refuge of good times and tasty things? After all, every other time I'd spent time with her I thought she was, yes, you know the rest. Capital T.

I engaged my soldier's brain and hatched a plan. I needed to escape. I had to escape from her. I had to do it now. I had identified several ball aches that would be a result of the Canadian's visit. Although in all truth, I just didn't want to clean up anymore sick. We'd just been taken over by a stray cat that we called Pepper Fanginton. He drank bleach and licked toxic oil pans at the garage near our flat and he preferred to empty his old messed up cat guts on our floor rather than the back alleys where he belonged.

Maybe, just maybe though, it's exactly what she needs. Who am I to stand so bare-faced in destiny's complicated plan? I shall become a retro shining knight and ride with her like the wind into a fairytale world of...

Nope! No! NO! NO! NO! NO! Get real, go home and go alone, go now. I can't even ride a horse. Set a time and run! There's no harm in running away. Thirty minutes in, the Canadian wasn't sure. Yes, I had an out.

"Actually you do look a bit peaky, maybe stay here eh?" Fall asleep, it's all a nightmare.

15 Minutes. "Nope, I'm good, I can walk." Shit!

10 Minutes. "Well I'm gunna go now so you know ...' Exit. Swift.

5 Minutes. "Just stay a bit longer." Those important moments.

1 Minute. "Mwah." I'm kissing Rose goodbye.

And the next minute I'm sat with a Canadian on a train. We glide over the river, the sun shining on one side, rain falling on the other. Somewhere in London people are pointing at the sky, saying 'Oh look! A rainbow!' like it's the most amazing and beautiful thing in the world. I turned my head towards the Canadian and thought exactly the same thing. After all, this girl was gunna be no trouble at all right?

She'd had drama. Some guy she was in love with had thrown her out of a pub. Cocaine arguments jizzed on with pints of lager. I decided that she needed to get away from the pretentious hot spots of East London and get some zone five calm. I suggested that she just move in with us. Why not? Adventure looms, and besides the 'some guy' obviously didn't want her around anymore. I pushed her suitcases with her through a summer storm. Her ripped jean shorts my only point of reference as we blinked our way to the bus stop. Two suitcases and a backpack. Simple. We spent the night smoking weed and drinking homemade cocktails. We shared a love of music and film.

"Oh my god, I fucking love that film, we gotta go!" Excitement.

She'd got tickets to a live orchestral performance of a Sundance winner. Barbican. Super cool. Something to look forward to.

"I think it's meant to be." Obviously.

"Nah mate, you're not her type." Builder's tea.

I had no idea what he meant. She liked films. I liked films. She liked music I liked music. I couldn't see how my flatmate didn't see that we were perfect for each other. She was fresh-faced and running from an intense relationship. Surely what she needed was a declaration of my eternal affection for her. To cheer her up and stuff. She'd only spent time in central London since she arrived. Bars, clubs and drugs were the sights. I held back. I didn't promise Christmas. I knew she'd be back in Canada by then. Instead I promised an English adventure. Up North to a real seaside. Mablethorpe. Home of real chips and fat ladies in wheelchairs. Home of colourful rock with words rolled in and donkey rides on the windy beach. What could be more British than that? We stayed up late singing duets on my guitar. Songs that were way too cool for me, but that let me sit next to her while she sang. It was intimate and musical. I was hypnotised. We stayed up until it got light. We talked about the things we loved and the things we wanted. I told her that I always want to scoop up hot lava from a volcano. She told me that she always wanted to hold a bird of prey. Something wild and free, something dangerous and transient. A hawk.

"I'll meet you for lunch before we go, I have a few things to do first." Show night. Good shoes.

We'd been living together now for two days. I was certain that there was a spark. She giggled and winked at me after each new verse and I played my heart out on my old guitar. I had to say something. Tony, my other housemate warned me.

"Don't do it. Don't tell her anything, you hardly know her, she needs a friend right now." Sensible.

When I arrived she'd already had two pints of Guinness and a big glass of wine. Tony was on a break from work and he'd joined us, contracted to a site up the road from Baker Street. Downing his pint he left us alone. The 'don't do it' look as steely as his kind old blue eyes. In for a cent.

"Do we need to have a talk?" Starting with a talk. Back to front logic.

"I know I've only know you for a few days ..." All the things I'd learned.

"Look, I'm just not ready for anything right now ..." She'd just been dramatically dumped.

"But, I feel it, don't you feel it?" We duet for fucks sake. What's wrong with you?

"Dude, I just wanna be friends, is that cool?" Booze. Neck. Down.

I went out for a ciggie. I was stunned. I was certain that something was pushing us together. The last vestige of romance teasing me with a final try at happiness. I hadn't been looking for someone new. I had come to the conclusion that I was better by myself. I was dizzy. Lunchtime pints. I smoked three before I went back in.

"This is awkward." Let's just high five.

"Hey, let's like totally bail on the bill!" Spice.

"Now?" Distraction from my embarrassment.

"Yeah, now!" Standing. Walking. Leg it!

We ran to the train station like naughty school kids pinching sweets from the corner shop. It was a while till the show and we were more than tipsy. She fell asleep on the train and dribbled down her chin as her platinum hair rolled and bobbed. I was completely in love with her and she'd told me to back off.

"Wake up lazy bitch, we're here." Gently shoving her awake.

The mood went strange. In the confusion of afternoon

drinks and badly timed declarations of affection we'd been locked out. Shit. The sun was bearing down and the booze was turning to narkiness.

"Why not? Come on? We'd be perfect?" Backing down was a coward's option.

"Dude, I just don't have feelings for you. I'm sorry!" Without her cocaine the drowsiness crept.

She kicked off her shoes and laid down on the steel platform at the top of our steps. I called my best friend Rose. I cried as I explained how much of a twat I felt. I was one-hundred-percent certain that this was all part of a bigger plan. What the actual fuck? It was practically a sin for us not to get together. We'd be the coolest couple in London. Singing, guitars and piano hip hop what else was there in life? When I finally let Rose go, the Canadian was asleep. The pints, the chat and my denial turning me less poetic.

"You're a fucking idiot woman, you gotta feel something?" Stupid boy.

Flipped. Switch. Anger. Shame.

"Fuck man, all I wanna do is get high! This is bullshit, I came here to get away from all the shit and you're being an asshole I can call my guy and have a gram here in twenty minutes if I want!" Harsh. Mainly true.

I thought that a dream romance would be the tonic she needed. Less than a week since she was ejected so violently and I was pissed off she didn't want to be my partner for life. I never once thought that she was taking us for a free ride. All the food, all the drinks, all the weed, all the time. Of course you can have it. Take it. Plug me in and inject everything I own into your lonely arms.

"Fine, fucking call him then, fuck off and get wasted, you stupid bitch!" I didn't say that. I did say that.

She bolted. Shouting at me how all she wanted was to get high. All she wanted to do was get down and dirty in a pub toilet with the Shoreditch druggeratti. All she wanted to do was smash her brains out so she didn't feel anything anymore. Fuck her. Go then. Ruin your life. Forget about the fish and chips by the sea and the bullshit folk songs I pretended to like. I don't need this any more than you do.

"She called me." All the bricks had run out. Tony was home.

I had a shower. I felt groggy after the afternoon piss up. I felt utterly foolish. She wouldn't answer my calls or my texts.

"I really wanted to see the show." I did. I wanted to see it with her.

She'd spoken to Tony. She was at the Barbican. I didn't know what to do. Be the better man. Go see the show. Enjoy each other as friends. He gave me twenty quid and I ran to get the train. If I hurried I'd make it in time. Five minutes out of the door she called me.

"Please be quick. If you don't get here soon ..." I'm going to get loaded. All the drugs.

She'd called her guy. He was twenty minutes away. When I arrived at the Barbican she sat by herself in a restaurant. Drinks only with food so there was an untouched plate in front of her and three empty bottles. She was steaming drunk. I felt like I'd saved her.

"Let's just have fun tonight, I'm sorry about all that

shit earlier, come on, this will be amazing." It will be. It was.

We took our seats and the lights went down. A full orchestra playing along with the film. It was moving. It was magical. The sounds of the instruments filling the room with vibrations that oozed through our bodies. I looked over. She was crying. The emotion of the music allowing her to let go. I wanted to take her hand. I wanted to put my arm around her and squeeze her, let her know I was there, let her know I understood. All I could do was hand her a tissue. After the show we took shots at the bar. She span and jumped to the tube station and we laughed.

"You're not actually that cool anyway." Bravado. Lies.

We became the annoying people on the train. It was hot. She spat water on me. I threw the Metro at her. Both of us pretending that all the drama of the day hadn't happened.

"What about tomorrow?" Mablethorpe. English chips.

"We'll see." Let's talk about it in the morning.

I went to bed, my head a bag of old chop suey and tequila. Instead of taking stock and heeding her flat out denial of love, I wondered. I wondered if after all these years, perhaps love was meant to be a fight. Nothing that good could come so easy. I was a fighter and a lover. I wasn't going to give up on her. I'd promised her sanctuary and all I did was trap her, fill her with anxiety and panic. Test. It's a test. I hoped she'd still come. The chances were low, but the smallest chance is the biggest beacon of light for a deluded dreamer.

When I woke up she was ready. Showered, packed, locked and loaded. Hope? We were going to spend the next four days together, alone in a place she'd never visited. Openly she told me she was worried.

"This might be a stupid idea." Platform two.

"Look, I promised tranquility, it'll be fun." Convincing myself.

As the view from the window turned from high rises to country houses, the weight of the weekend sat on my head like a fat woman. I had no idea what would happen. I knew that I had to keep my advances to myself, back off with the love shit dude. On the way to my Mum's house we stopped at Jonny and Helen's. Two of the best people you'll ever meet. We had cups of tea and she took photos of their beautiful kids playing in the garden. Taking pictures was her passion. The immaculately cute kids providing all the poses you could ever want.

"She's nuts mush. Perfect for you." My old best buddy wanting the best for me. Hopeful arms wrapped around me like Chewbacca.

I had new hope. My reality was tempted. I told myself to rely on facts not fantasy. What did I know? I knew she was alone in a foreign country and with a man she'd only known for a matter of weeks. I knew she liked a drink.

"Gin?" Fridge full of tonic.

We spent the night swapping songs. Her taste was cool. My taste was pop. More drinks. More songs. She span around in my Mum's living room and she looked free.

"Shooting stars!" Away from the city lights the sky gave us fireworks.

We climbed into the back of one of my Stepdad's flatbed trucks in the yard. Countryside darkness. No lights and no neighbours. We pulled corks and wrapped ourselves up in blankets and watched the universe twinkle.

In the morning she made tequila sunrises without the tequila. Head groggy from the night before she told me she was anxious. Nervous. Something she dealt with. Something in her head. I had a great idea. A good old bit of Benny Hill humour to lighten the mood. It would go like this. I'd call her to the bottom of the stairs.

1. I'd flash her in my beach towel and do a silly dance.

2. She'd think it was hilarious and laugh.

She hadn't heard of Benny Hill. The familiar kazoo theme music wasn't ringing in her head as I whipped away my towel in the hope of a post card chuckle. Not one bit. Instead I'd punched a large red button with the words 'Panic' on it. Balls. I'd fucked up. I'd always thought I was pretty funny. Now I was scrambling to make my apologies and explain my actions. Over a half-eaten cooked brunch I needed to clear the air.

"I'm really sorry about earlier." I was only trying to make her laugh.

"I'm in your Mother's house away from anyone I know, in a place where I've never been, I'm on my own and you show me your cock." Zero comedy points to me.

Whoops.

"Let's get out and about, bit of fresh air. There's a castle! That's pretty English." Tourist board cheese aversion.

It started to rain. As we walked through the grounds to

the castle wall, a wedding party tried to make the most of their big day. I laughed. We sat and looking over the wall onto the countryside. Even in the rain it's beautiful. She started to cry.

"You'll just end up hating me, they all do." The Canadian opened up like the sky.

"I'll never hate you." Because of course I'm not like them, I'm special. Needs.

She told me that all the guys she ever meets tell her they love her. That they all start out as friends then get weird. Her playful nature and rock chic attitude dangling like a carrot in front of anyone with a pulse. I asked if any had flashed her a badly timed knob. I wanted to be special. Her personality on the outside was attractive. Confident and exciting. Drugs, rock, roll and everything else. A firework on a grey afternoon. Transient and adventurous. Exactly the kind of girl I always wanted. I wanted her even more when I saw her cry. It's a chemical thing. Clutching her chest, she said she wanted to walk. It was all getting too much. I was hoping that being strong for her would see that I was Mister Right. I chose my words carefully. Mentally editing everything I said to make me sound compassionate and caring. Understanding. What a guy. Changing what I really felt and lying to her face to make the situation better.

"I need to sleep. I need to lay down." Short of breath.

Anxiety. Walls closing in on her. I asked what sparked off her panic attack.

"You did ..." Ah. Fair point.

Walking back to the car I thought that a short sharp

shock would take her mind off things. I kept my cock in my pants this time and jumped onto an empty market stall and sang as loud as I could,

"Why do you build me up, butter cup baby, just to let me down." Then mess me around.

I got a smile. She became lighter. Her hand moved away from her throat. She thanked me for a public display of stupidity. It worked. I wanted to explain that the whole flash your balls jape was similar in intent but I decided to leave it alone. Wanting to close her eyes and just be still, I suggested we drive back to my Mum's house. She fell asleep. Snoring and curled up in the back like a street urchin.

"English as fuck!" Village cricket.

I'd driven the long way. I'd known that restless babies like to be driven around to help them relax. While she dozed, the sun came out. When she opened her eyes she was looking at grown men dressed in white, chasing a red ball around a field. A few of the locals had picnics. Wise old folk mixing with the next generation. All creatures, great and small. We stayed for half an hour. Not saying much. Watching the lazy cricket. Sky blue, no sign of stormy weather.

"I think I have something wrong with me." Western diagnosis for her addled brain.

"Nothing that a trip to the seaside won't fix." They did it in the old days. Sprung. Eternal.

I knew that she had a dream, something she told me she always wanted to do. Something on a list. A list of incredible things. Somehow, I had to make it happen.

There was a small sanctuary on the East coast near a tiny seaside town called Mablethorpe. Perfect. We watched Hugh Grant in my Mum's posh telly room and went to bed early.

"Fuuuuuck dude! You nearly hit that car!" Panic button. Three metres from the driveway.

The first two minutes of our trip had almost set her off, back into her dark world of headphones, self-loathing and guitar music. At least the sun was shining. It was a glorious day. The roads lined with bright yellow rapeseed and Windows desktop background relaxed her. We stopped halfway. There were bulls in a field and she wanted to take pictures of them. I needed a piss. She skipped down the tree-lined roads and sat on the electric fence. Come on. A day like this. Blue sky. Sunshine. Just me and her. Surely? Tony's advice was to just have a good time, enjoy each other, don't push anything because,

"She DON'T like you that way fella!" Any clearer and he'd be invisible.

A large bunch of molecules in my body that could just about hear Tony were telling me that she wasn't interested. A large bunch of molecules were telling the others to fuck right off. Molecular battles. Stupid building blocks, what do they know? This girl was worth the fight. Never give up. We were in good spirits when we arrived at the seal sanctuary. By the time we got there it was late in the afternoon.

"God, they look so depressed." Animal mood swings. Mood slides. A playpark of moods.

I had to agree with her to some extent. The place was

more a dirty lay-by with a pool full of knackered fat animals than a sanctuary.

"Better than being bludgeoned in front of your pups for meat and moccasins though?" Bright side.

We spent an hour wandering around and laughing at the displays. Blue Peter and low budgets. I didn't think that the sabre tooth tiger skull was real. I could see where they glued the teeth on. It didn't matter.

While she was taking pictures of their big wild birds, I slipped off and found the manager.

"No way at all? Even if I give you a bunch of money? How much do you want?" Negotiations.

My plan was to get a bird of prey on her arm. I wanted to make an actual dream come true. I decided that even if I wasn't her type, even if she didn't fancy me, even if she'd just been dumped, that making a little dream a reality would prove that I was the man for her.

"They're wild, probably go for her eyes." Rescue birds.

Thematic. I'd tried to rescue them all. Scuppered at the post. Damn it. Now she will never fall in love with me.

"There is a bird centre a few miles away from here, but they'll be shut in half an hour." Get ready.

The lovely lady who didn't want us to get our eye pecked out gave me a number. I rang it instantly.

"He's putting the birds away for the day now, you can come back tomorrow?" Teenage. Weekend job.

I implored that this was important. I span a yarn. I explained that I'd made a bet with my new Canadian girlfriend, who was very much in love with me, that If I could get a picture of a hawk on her arm and upload it to Instagram by the time it got dark that she'd stay with me in London, where she belonged, instead of going back home when her visa expired. It was a matter of life and death, our paths may never cross again, I needed to get the bird.

"What's your number? Let me try and find the boss …" Hang up.

The seal sanctuary manager had told me it was a fifteen-minute drive, if you knew the way. I had no idea where it was and no sat nav. It was twenty minutes until they closed and I hadn't even spoken to anyone with authority. Concede. Let it go. Maybe it wasn't right after all. Perhaps the signs that I'd searched for in the details were just in my head. Everywhere I looked I saw weddings, romance. Connecting horoscope trivia and songs about falling in love played in passing cars extra loud so I could hear. I thought the universe had sent her. Illusions hiding delusions. On a stormy wet afternoon, I stole her from London's trendy drug addicts. I told her I loved her after three days, and after she flatly said 'No', I drove her hundreds of miles to the coast in the middle of England and tried to make her bird of prey dream come true. I was a huge massive joke. This was never going to work. Not in a million years. I'd created my very own Mills and Boon sadistic story…

"Hello? Someone said summink about Hugh Grant or summink?" Bad signal. The boss called back.

I explained the story. If I can just get a bird of prey on her arm. Boom. It was half true. I thought if I could actually make this work, all my effort and fast talking would prove my affections for her.

"The rest of my love life is in your hands, screw romcoms, this is real, real life, all I need is a single bird of prey, one arm, one picture, one minute, do you want to be part of something truly wonderful?" Laid on thicker then Northern mushroom gravy.

"If you can get here in fifteen minutes I'll see what I can do." Half-believing. The heavens were smiling.

Shit. Fifteen minutes. Shit. No sat nav. Shit. Phone about to die. Shit. I drive like a grandma. I'd been given a chance, no turning back now. If I did, I'd be lost anyway. With one minute to go I pulled into the farm. Fifteen minutes but a thousand miles away from the seal sanctuary. Open space. Farm house style. Tea shop at the gates and a line of six people. Teenage weekend workers all waiting to see if we were real or a lame hoax call. They cheered as we opened the car doors and ran to the first barn. A kind-faced gentleman in hunting gear and a huge leather glove was waiting for us, and there it was.

"I called her Cleo." After his first wife. Beautiful, flighty and never shut's up.

He'd picked out his favourite. A massive Canadian Hawk.

"I didn't think you guys were real!" A little excitement before closing for the day.

We had to keep up the pretense. For half-an-hour we were a couple. All eyes were on us as the staff wanted to know if she was going to stay or leave.

"You'll have to kiss me now." Peck on the cheek. For all my efforts.

The generous expert told us all about his prized bird.

How he'd had to spend thousands on her visa. How he'd reared her from an early age. He let us feed her and flew her over our heads. The flap of the wings cooling us down in the scorching sun. I took my photo. Everyone clapped. For a few minutes I'd made someone's dream come true. The look on her face was worth it. She was excited about something that wasn't sold in small paper wraps. I felt like a hero.

I parked the car by the Mabletherpe beach. Strolled amongst the electric wheelchair smokers and sunburnt plumbers on the annual fortnight off. Sulky teenagers secretly texting their holiday flings and little kids fucked up on candy floss and cheap pop. We played arcade games and air hockey, swapping tickets for rub-on tattoos. The pubs looked dodgy. The typical east coast dives, decorated by a blind man in the sixtiess but full of life and stories. Families. Real families. Grandmas with sherry and grandkids with shandy.

"Karaoke mother fucker!" Half a lemonade for the driver and a pint for the lady.

It was hilarious. The singing had just started when we stepped through the alleyway past the hand- written sign. Dad's doing their best Robbie Williams while embarrassed but loving daughters tried to ignore the paternal hip thrusts aimed firmly at mum. Everly Brothers. Dolly Parton. Eagles. You name it, they sang it. The Canadian whose dream had just come true wanted to get in the mix.

"Nelly, you got Nelly, he's a rapper, you got any rap music?" Accent causing the DJ to scratch his head.

With the opening bars. The room full of locals and fat

friendly holiday makers all span around to see what was about to happen. Her platinum blonde hair, black roots and denim swagger were as out of place as her song choice. She spat bars. This time no piano, Sun Fly providing the on screen lyrics. The seventies providing the sound system.

"Oh why must I feel this way? Must be the money!" I sang the chorus.

We smashed it. More applause. Everywhere we went we were surround by people clapping. We made friends. A lovely lady called Sue invited us to sit with them. Pensioners spending their days drinking, singing and laughing.

"Ooh, you two are fabulous. Touch of pizzazz, just what this place needs, how long have you been together?" Open faced, genuine soul.

I turned to the Canadian rapper. This would be the perfect time to relinquish. The perfect time to give in to my efforts.

"It's complicated." Big chug of Stella Artois.

Sue offered us a room in her house. Stay and get drunk. A hefty biker tested our musical knowledge. Questions about obscure musicians. He was impressed at her knowledge. It was more Hi-De-Hi than Benny Hill, luckily. A time-hole throwback. The jeans were tight on their legs because they were fat. The beards we full of chips and beans not stylish irony.

"Don't go yet! Do one more, give us song." Sing one for her.

I dropped my old faithful, 'I just called to say I love you' by Mr Wonder. Sue told me with wink that I'd sang it for her. I laughed and told her I'd tried my best. I'd made one of her dreams come true and like Winehouse she was still saying no, no, no.

As we hugged our new friends goodbye the day was coming to an end. I'd noticed a sign that said sunset car park so I swung by. The beach was completely empty. The sun setting with a hazy glow. The waves gently crashing.

"Let's go for a splash!" I'd just learned to swim. No trunks.

"Last one in's a frikken doosh bag!" Bag on the floor. No towels.

The water was warm. Warm compared to how I imagined it would be. I got there first. There were only the two of us in the whole ocean. The sky changing minute by minute. Blue to pink to red. The water gently caressing our bodies as we stood alone face to face.

"This would be a perfect time to kiss." I knew the answer would be no.

"Yes." One word. Heartbeat. Then she turned away.

We drove home in soggy pants and dresses, accompanied by two hours of cheese courtesy of Magic FM. We grabbed a cheeseburger from the roundabout near my Mum's house and she went to bed. Worn out from the day, the weekend, the week, the whole of her life. So many perfect moments, but none of them good enough to melt her maple heart.

"We would make a great couple. You're a Mom pleaser." Second pint before the train back to London.

"You can't argue with your Mum." With a 'U'. I knew what she meant.

We spent the next few days smoking weed and playing guitar till late. Listening to music. One afternoon I get an e-mail from an old producer friend. He's got a song signed to Ministry of Sound but they don't like the vocal. He asks me if I'd lay a few ideas over the track. As soon as I heard it I thought it needed an American-sounding female rap. Kapow. I quickly wrote a verse and asked the Canadian to record it. I sent it over and he loved it but they wanted a male lead. I thought he was wrong. The track sounded super heavy in her husky drugged out drawl so I floated it to Ian and David, my gay-not-gay music compadres from the old days. Ian thought we should do our own version. I agreed. I told the Canadian that we'll be recording in a few days.

"Holy shit! I have stars in my eyes!" Indie music, electro rave. All the same.

The studio is in Shoreditch so she ties in a little reunion with her old late night pals. I start to worry. I know she has an addictive personality and I know that her friends will all have the sniffles. Passing the little pub on the way to the train station into town she's thirsty. We pop in and she orders a couple of ciders. We down them and then she picks up two cans of gin and tonic. We neck the lot on the train, it's only ten in the morning. By the time we get there I'm tiddly. We smash the vocal in an hour. It flows as easy as the booze.

"Matey, that sounds fucking sweet!" Unique Kid.

When we leave the session it's almost dinner time. She can get half-price food at the Rivington where she worked. Bonus. There is such thing as a free lunch. While we wait for our duck liver pate she pops to the toilet via an old face. We order a couple of cocktails, on the house. There is such a thing as a free drink too.

"Dude, it's like full of fucking ice man!" The English don't complain. The Canadian did.

I'm not one to look a gift horse in the arse but I noticed a slight gurn. I noticed the vacant look in her eyes and the haste in which she wanted to tell the manager that the drinks were watered down. Within minutes she was swaying. Over-excited about the prospect of seeing all the people that she wanted to escape from.

"It was just a bump dude, if you don't like it you don't have to stay." One line now, one for later?

I didn't like it. I left. Fuck this. Watching someone you care about switch from genuine creative glee to chemical-induced fascination made me feel sick. I'd done more than my fair share of drugs in the Nineties but I didn't want to see a beautiful girl chew her cheeks off over our starter. It was a couple of days before she came back. The lustre had gone. Her lips dry and cracked and her eyes ice cold and paranoid. She spent hours in front of her laptop listening to music, ears full of orange headphones and eyes full of tears. Showers and deodorant become a thing of the past and her ear gets infected. After a week of trying to help her, feeding her jelly beans and making sure she ate at least a nibble we ended up at the local hospital. I brought my skate board as there was a park opposite the A&E. Great place for a mini ramp. You can slam hard and crawl to the emergency room. After her fiasco of a diagnosis we sit in the park in the sun. I skin up and she pops an ollie. Amusing. I'd always wanted a wife who could skateboard, although without the manky ear and the drug addiction.

She ends up staying out more and more. Each time coming home stinking of BO and cans of lager. Each time slamming her door and locking herself in her room. I try to communicate. She's wary of me. I understand.

"Really? Nothing at all. Not even a tiny little bit?" I couldn't believe it. My ego was being bummed hard.

It's hard. Having to see her every day. Watching her dissolve into the monster she hated so much when she escaped the clutches of the ironic uber cool.

"I should move out, but I'll only go if you ask me." Finally, an out.

"Stay, I'll be cool, I promise." As empty as her soul.

I know that the right thing to do is get her to move out. We were draining each other like vampires. There was no way that we'd ever get together, not now. I went from cocky dream-maker to crying in my bedroom like a love-sick teenage girl.

"I'll never fall in love with you, and I'll never fuck you." Black and white.

I resorted to putting black ink dots on my feet to remind me what she said. One for 'love' and one for 'fuck'. I'd analyse every syllable of the nonsense conversations we had for any sign of hope. Any sign that secretly she did love me and this was all a very intricate and fucking torturous test. Richard O'Brian's 'Crystal Meth Maze'. She was spending more and more time at the pub. Each night coming back drunk. All the spirits in the house one by one emptied themselves and threw themselves in the bin. Chucking the cat shit out one night in the neighbour's bin I found bags and bags of empty booze cans. If there were any more beers, an enterprising Pakistani family would have opened a shop. It was too much. I knew that there was no hope. No romance. No love. There was simply nothing I could do. Some people are just not made for each other. The daily reminder of her living at our house was making me insane.

I knew I needed to get out of the house more. Not waste my days waiting for a pissed up girl who would never 'love' or 'fuck' me. My two dots a constant. I'd taken time away from my acting class. A mental five hours with my two mentors Bryan and Eva was too much to take, as much as I loved it's frankly batshit craziness, I was in no fit mental state to handle it. Eva had put me together with an actress who was looking to shoot a little piece after a little time out of the scene. Something for her showreel. Something for mine. I'd neglected all aspects of my life that didn't revolve around a non- starting love affair with a tattooed Moose-lover. It was a great scene, from Frankie & Johnny and the Claire De Lune. One day a week. I jumped on it. Something to take my mind off my fantasy nightmare. One pretend scenario for another. At least I would know how one of them ended. Flip to the last page. No uncertainty there.

We did our first session on the top of a tree in Hyde Park where the Lost Boys slept. I'd always known it as the inspiration for Peter Pan and I hadn't really thought it through as I asked the returning actress to climb to the top with me in her floaty summer dress. She was intense, kind and giving. Everything an actor needs. She also liked a gossip.

"She's taking the piss out of you!" Compassion. Tree tops.

"I know but I just can't stop thinking about her, every minute of every day." Any ear. Any excuse.

She bollocked me for sticking up for her at every opportunity. I had to defend her. I knew that the Canadian was troubled. It wasn't her fault I told her I loved her after seventy-two hours. It wasn't her fault that I couldn't ask her to leave. All that free rent, booze, weed, travel and food. It must have been hard for her to stay. The Canadian had been spending more and more time at the pub. Her part-time job paying for her daily tab rather than the money that she, by now, owed us all. My other house mate Mike couldn't give a shit if she went back to Canada. She'd never talked to him and mostly blanked him. He'd expressed a non-interest in her from the beginning. Her charms didn't work on old Mikey boy, he preferred a more 'refined' lady and besides he had about four women on the go. The tension in the house was unbearable. The vibe was ruined. Once a house of noisy dinners at the table and jam sessions on anything. Now a house of slamming doors, stolen liquor and folk music sobs. Everything that the Canadian and I talked about was careful. I could feel her editing her sentences. I just wanted to scream that I loved her but I swallowed it and it became a lukewarm stream of agreeableness covered with bullshit. I stopped eating so much. My guts in knots. I stopped sleeping so much, my brain in tatters.

"You look terrible!" My tree top actress was all about honesty.

I'd lost weight. Which I didn't mind, it meant that I didn't have to go to the gym, but I could feel the burden of my own foolish actions burning deep dark circles in my eyeballs.

"You're obsessed with her and she's nothing but bad news." Smash me with a brick.

I was obsessed. I knew for a fact that nothing would happen. But for some strange reason there was a razorblades chance that it would all just change. A universal reset button where I'd wake up and the dry-nosed Canadian would be cooking me raspberry pancakes and doing Pilates in the living room.

"You're an idiot, you're missing the world!" Heartache, bogies and puke. "If you don't snap out of it you might miss the girl of your dreams standing right in front of you!" Summer dress by Chloe. Richard Curtis pep talk.

Maybe she was right. I needed to get away from the Canadian. I felt bad, I couldn't kick her out because I'd convinced her to move in. Her visa was up in a couple of months, but eight weeks would feel like a lifetime. I needed to get as far away as possible. I put the word out. I needed to disappear. Make some money, get my head straight. Crashing towards forty years old and lying awake night after night wondering if the girl who said she 'hated everything I love' would realise that in fact, she didn't.

Brent, who had spent the last decade marrying Americans in upstate New York had been playing with radio control cars and he was good. He'd seen an opportunity and had decided to start a little business with drone cams. With my production experience, he threw me a bone.

"Get ya arse out here, you cunt, make some fucking money and forget that bitch, you ain't even shagged her anyway!" Best friends cut to the chase.

It was perfect. He'd got a job filming on a golf course that would pay for my ticket out there. It was only a few weeks away, all I had to do was keep my cool and ignore the Canadian. Simple. Effective, and just in time. I'd lost almost a stone and a half and hadn't slept properly for months.

"She's a twat mate, get off to New York, do you good." Old school advice. Kettle.

Matt, who owned the little gallery below our house had seen me transform. Since my romantic demise he'd given me little jobs to do to keep me occupied. His wife Sarah had said to him that she didn't trust her from the beginning. Pepper the cat didn't like her either. We had a cup of tea, milky, one sugar. I was so glad to be leaving. It was the only thing that kept me from having a massive panic attack.

"Job's gone balls-up mate, not gunna be able to get the ticket for ages." Face-Time sorries.

Shit. Faced with another two months of the Canadian my brain snapped. My body shook and trembled in my bed while Tony sat with me and let me wail. He always came to the rescue. A bricklayer by trade, a saint by nature. It was horrible. I couldn't open my eyes. I couldn't breathe. Every single one of my romantic mistakes came flooding back to me. The blueberries for Claire. Every other nasty selfish romantic excuse for a row. The secret in the broken bag. All at once. Kicking the little blue car. I was nearly middle-aged and sobbing my heart out, frozen solid with a tradesman by my side. Things hadn't gone to plan.

"Fresh air mate. Walk to town, get some fags, pull ya socks up." Chirpy. Solid. Salt. Earth.

The walk did me good. I laughed. I laughed hard for the first time in weeks. One foot in front of the other and a dictionary's worth of bad building site jokes. Just what I needed. When I got back the Canadian wasn't there, she'd gone out for a drink. I had to face facts, this was going to be tough, I had tried to escape but reality had punched me in the balls and I'd fought back. I didn't mention what had happened as she came in. I offered her a joint instead. Then things went weird.

"I can't breathe!" Stammering, falling, floor.

The Canadian was having a panic attack. Clutching at her throat and scrambling for air I was freaked out. Just four hours earlier I had done exactly the same thing. She sobbed hard. Froze on the floor. I couldn't deal with it. I didn't want to help her, my physical contact being so contracted and carefully selected I didn't want to even touch her. She was crumbling on the floor in front of me and all I could do was watch. For the first time in ages I slept.

The next day I woke to find her on the old Chesterfield. She was groggy. She was slow. We'd both had a panic attack on the same day. She'd said to me before that I was the only person who could get her out of one of her moods, I'd sang Motown classics to brighten her gloom many times by now.

"Let's go swimming! Come on, I'll show you my new

dive!" I'd just learned how to swim.

Reluctantly, she agreed. The summer's day warming us both. Fresh start. Forget this love shit. I'll never mention it again. I showed her my dive. It was new for me, I was excited. We left the pool and walked through the park to dry off. The chat was light. The chat was positive. I told her I was sorry for all the pressure and the insane obsession. She told me it was okay, it was just that she, "Wasn't in a place to have any kind of relationship with a guy at the minute." Sun-dried blonde.

When we got back we were both in a better mood. We laughed about the time she borrowed some money and bought fireworks for Mike's birthday and she taught us how to shoot them into the air with our hands. Things were calm, things were good. We high-fived as she went to work. Late shift. She'd text me when she finished, she'd lost her key again.

"I'll steal some nibbles from the pub." Crisps and nuts. There is such a thing as a free snack.

The phone rang. My agent Tom. He'd got me a casting for a new film starring Johnny Depp. I had sides to learn. Thank you, universe. Time to get back in the game.

"I'm going out with the girls, I'll be back tomorrow." Girls. She always said she never got on with girls. Fishy.

Something about the text didn't feel right. I knew she was with a guy. I knew she was up to something. She wasn't my girlfriend. I knew this but I wanted to know. Whether I had a right to or not I replied.

Nothing. No reply. I called her. I had to know. Nothing. I spent the next twelve hours stressing out. Who was it?

Why had she lied? Fucking bitch! I couldn't sleep. My mind inventing the worst scenarios. Her and her fuck buddy laughing about the sad middle-aged man who thought he could tame a rock chic. I knew she had drugs in her room. A doctor's visit and a bag of tears had earned her a strip of downers. I banged four of them in the hope I'd sleep. I wanted to work with Depp. I just wanted to know.

"Let me in." Nine in the morning.

"Look, I know it's not my business, but were you with a ..." Rage. Humiliation.

She pushed past me and slammed her door shut. I started to shake. Anger building up, a valve exploding as all of my stupidity and obsession could no longer remain inside my ragged body. She came out, her eyes cold and beaten, her nose red, her lips cracked like the rim of a margarita.

"Yeah so what, I've been seeing a guy from work, it's not your business!" The truth hurts. I broke.

Without turning back to look at her I fired my full force into the world.

"You got ten seconds to get your shit and fuck off or I'll FUCKING BURN EVERYTHING YOU OWN!"

I had a lighter. I had a temper.

She ran out of the house. I didn't care. For the first time ever Pepper the cat came and sat on my lap and went to sleep. I couldn't move. Frozen by rage and a stray old tabby. Depp. Casting. Shit. Shower. I went to the audition. I didn't get the job. The casting director said that I'd scared her. Fuck it. I rang my film partner Robin and he told me to come and see them in Hitchin. Dinner, friends, safe place. I played picnics with his little girl who wanted to dress up like a pumpkin and ate a delicious meal cooked by his wife Sara. When I got back home. Her room was empty. She was gone. I exhaled. I breathed out for the first time. For the first time in almost twenty-eight years I was neither falling in love or heart broken. I was nothing. Romance I decided, was well and truly dead.

18.

I slept. I ate. I breathed. I went back to class. I smiled. Some of my friends thought I was a dick for what I did. No I wouldn't have burned her clothes. Yes, I handled it badly. Nothing new to be honest. I'd handled each and every one of my relationships the only way I knew how. Always with a promise of perfection. Always with a promise of the dream come true. I wanted to entice, rescue, impress, discover, convince, entertain, devour. Time to stop. Not long until my fortieth birthday. I'd achieved a lot, seen a lot and wanted to share it all. Now, I was tired. Tired of it all. I was serene in my singledom. Dreams of a little girl I'd name 'Poppy' and the most beautiful ballerina wife turned into a thoughtful chuckle, a sharp intake of air and a knowing tut tut tut. Some people are just not meant to be in a relationship, no matter how hard they try. No matter what delicious efforts they go to. No matter how much they think they deserve happiness. Happiness didn't lie in obsession. Happiness wasn't in grand sweeping gestures. Happiness was in the little things. I accepted this. I was okay with this. I threw myself back into learning. My old alumni filling me with energy and a focus. It was a shame that my mum would never have a grandchild from me and my little lady. She could pin her genetic nanny dreams on my little brother and his acrobatic girlfriend. Their kids would be vivacious enough.

The sun faded after a long hot and weird summer and turned slowly into tinsel and adverts for toys. Christmas was coming. The goose was looking hefty.

"I'm never inviting anyone else for Christmas ever, ever again." But I'll be there for the roast potatoes. More for me.

I always loved roast potatoes. I still do. Everyone knows someone who makes the best. Best in the street, best in the family. Each one different. Each one unique. Crispy on the outside. Fluffy in the middle. Par boiled. Shaken in a pan. Goose fat. Duck butter. Only turn once. Dollop of Marmite. Only turn twice. Heat the pan for an hour first. Just a pinch of salt. The perfect flavour.

"We're not having a big roast this year anyway ..." My Mum's special birthday was the day after Boxing day.

I spent Christmas day with my brother Martin, his girlfriend Hannah and my Dad in good old Leeds. The stunt team and the Kung Fu crew all came around and we had a Chinese steam boat, scallops, prawns and strips of tasty bacon. Not a crispy Maris Piper in sight. I'd mentioned that it was my Mum's birthday to some of my acting friends at the pub after class before I left for the North.

"The more the merrier!" The gin will flow.

My brother and I had made her a music video celebrating her life and the people that loved her and the things she loved. I'd asked Eva to do a little bit to camera after class one evening. We even managed to get our ninety-seven-year-old Grandad to dance in the music video. He had more groove in his boots than some of my uncles and a far stronger bladder. A few minutes before we were about to surprise our Mum in front of two hundred merry people my phone rang.

"I'm here!" Car phone speakers.

Green dress, long shiny dark hair. Ballerina poise. Ruby red lips. My actress friend. The girl from the top of the tree. She'd told me that she didn't really like Christmas. The last few years for her and her Dad had been tough. I'd mentioned my Mum's party in class a week before. She didn't have plans for the invisible week between Christmas Eve and New Year's Day. Wanting as much as possible to be cheerful. I'd said to her,

"Why not come along, there's gunna be Elvis, Karaoke and a surprise!" Not the real Elvis, but he was pretty good. No open fires, no country house. Just the King of Rock.

I didn't think she'd come. I hadn't double checked. I was way too busy to think about who was coming and who wasn't. My brother and I were up to our eyes in steaming chilli fish balls and video edit suites until the morning of the party. I'd sent her the postcode and left it at that. I was impressed that she found the venue. I was impressed when all the drunk Dads turned their heads out of eyeshot of their even drunker wives and checked out her ballerina figure. I was impressed when the drunk wives winked at me when they saw her designer shoes.

"I probably won't stay." Got to get back for the dog.

It was late. All the booze drunk and just the hardcore left in the building doing cartwheels and handstands in front of the DJ as he packed up his disco lights.

"You can sleep in my bed. I'll make a pillow wall!" Totally safe. Impenetrable feathers. She stayed the night.

19.

I'd spent a few months with the ballerina from the tree top. Taking it easy. Enjoying the ride. Long enough for the summer to roll around again. My big bad birthday was looming. The big four-oh-fuck. I didn't want a big party. I just wanted to go skateboarding with my moody old mate Jay and my little Brother. My Mum had offered to pay for a trip to the Midi Pyrenees the week after. A lovely little house in St Lizier. The brochure called it the most beautiful village in France. I'd had visions of at least someone on my arm when I turned forty. At least the sniff of the faintest idea of a smidgen of the pitter patter of tiny wheels. I settled for a private dance. My private dancer. My ballerina tree top girl. She'd made my favourite cake, a black forest gateaux made from scratch. I wore a shirt and tie to the skatepark. My brother wore knee pads, elbow pads, hip guard and a helmet. He face-planted after dropping in a seven-foot ramp and bit through his lip. The only part of his body that wasn't padded. I lasted about forty minutes until the warehouse turned yellow and everyone started talking in echoes. One minute for every year I'd been alive. One minute for every year I'd been chasing girls. Searching endlessly for the perfect roast potato. I had to sit down. I was about to pass out. Not wanting to be left out of the extreme sports fun, my ballerina tree top cake baker did a pirouette on a mini ramp. It was funny. I really liked it.

A week later I was in St Lizier. My best friend Rose was reading a book about clever monkeys. Her mate Yana, a five-foot-ten Czechoslovakian interior designer was floating on a child's inflatable jet ski, and I was watching the sun set over the mountains with the girl from the top of the tree. We argued on the last night, but we'd made up by the next day. She made me jump in the pool naked. Five times. It worked.

I stayed at my Mum's house after we got back from France. I needed a break from London and a break from the debt collectors. It seemed like I had a girlfriend and I hadn't even tried. I hadn't promised anything, apart from Elvis Presley. The tree-top ballerina that made me my favourite cake was calling me her 'sausage'. Not a vegetarian. One- hundred percent meat eater.

"We're taking Granddad to lunch, you can drive, so I can have a drink." My Mum's not an alcoholic. She just finds it refreshing.

I asked my Granddad to record a video for me when we'd pottered out for a roll up after his pie and mash.

"What's the secret to a happy life." Gizza light old fella.

"Get married. Especially to that lass, I like her, I think she's a nice girl." Decades of life. Thick rich Cricklewood accent.

"You gunna dance at our wedding then?" He used to cha cha.

"I can't dance but I can shuffle." With age comes wisdom. And new hips.

In a couple of years, my Granddad will be one hundred

years old. More than anything I want to see him dance at our wedding. Whether it's a cha cha, a rumba, a twerk, or like he said, a 'shuffle'. I think I'd better get a move on and ask her.

I wonder what she'll say?

Author photo by Mimi Dendias

SIMON WAN spent his early life dodging detentions and falling in love all over the UK and Ireland. His love for girls is matched by his love of cats, skateboards, food, music and robots.

A post university adventure in pop music took him to the strangest night clubs and festivals and his adventures in film making took him all over the world.

Simon recently took to stage and screen and attained international acclaim with nominations and awards for his performances in British Kung Fu film drama "Dog" and stage production "Mr Foo" with Tina Malone.

He has now decided to become author because he can write books wearing just a towel and he can type really fast.

"*A promise of relentless energy, noise, a lot of madness and probably a lot of drugs, which luckily is exactly what Simon Wan delivers – bar the drugs*"
RANKIN

"*He goes way beyond passion*"
FEARNE COTTON

"*The guy's energy is incredible. I just wish I had his hair*"
LIMAHL

"*I said he should write a book, and he did*"
EVA POPE

Urbane Publications is dedicated to developing new author voices, and publishing fiction and non-fiction that challenges, thrills and fascinates.

From page-turning novels to innovative reference books, our goal is to publish what YOU want to read.

Find out more at

urbanepublications.com